THE WHITE BIRD

LAURAN PAINE

SAGEBRUSH
Large Print Westerns

First published in Great Britain by Gunsmoke
First published in the United States by Five Star

First Isis Edition
published 2016
by arrangement with
Golden West Literary Agency

A catalogue record for this book is available
from the British Library.

ISBN 978–1–78541–212–7 (pb)

Published by
F. A. Thorpe (Publishing)
Anstey, Leicestershire

Set by Words & Graphics Ltd.
Anstey, Leicestershire
Printed and bound in Great Britain by
T. J. International Ltd., Padstow, Cornwall

This book is printed on acid-free paper

THE WHITE BIRD

Though elderly buffalo hunter Sam Sloan doesn't know when he sets out on his quest for a spirit vision and a final resting place, something is drawing him towards a fateful meeting — a meeting that is destiny. Many-Horses, a Navajo, is near death from starvation when Sloan encounters him in the forest, but recuperates as he assists the old hunter with the construction of a log cabin. Then White Magpie, a Sioux escapee from Crow Indian captivity, arrives, accompanied by the young girl Yellow Bluebell; and Sloan discovers gold in a nearby creek. But disaster is looming — a white bird foretells it in a dream . . .

27.

CHAPTER
ONE

A Minor Mystery

There were burned rocks in small circles. There were also scarcely distinguishable teepee rings where hide houses had once stood. Otherwise there was no sign. If there had been tracks to the creek and back, they had been long since obliterated by rains, snow, and time. Now there were only stories — there were always stories, usually embroidered, untrue but colorful. In the nearest town, Boulder, a thriving community whose sources of sustainable income derived from cattle and the railroad, the stories became legends.

A few old gaffers remembered Boulder as the collection point for dun-colored hides in bales and, later, bones, huge piles of buffalo bones to be shipped by railroad to Eastern reduction factories where they were pulverized and sold as fertilizer. Eventually the enormous piles of bones were depleted as were the bales of hides because the sources of both had been almost completely eliminated. Now, only small bands of buffalo remained, no longer lords of the plains, furtive, wary creatures at the mercy of men on fast horses who killed them on sight for sport.

Men like William F. Cody who at one time killed nearly four hundred head to feed railroad crews had gone on to better, more lucrative things. What they left behind was huge areas of grassland for the next generation, the cattlemen. Yet, if the great herds were gone, what remained were haunting winds and an occasional scattering of bleached bones of large shaggy animals who had learned how to survive terrible winters, now replaced by domestic horned critters who depended on hay stacks and those who made them to survive.

Sam Sloan, who had contributed to the slaughter as a professional buffalo hunter, told the saloonman in Boulder that he had believed the millions of "bufflers" were an inexhaustible source, ready for the killing. Then he made a wry smile before he said the rest of it. "They're gone, maybe, an' I don't feel good about my part in it."

Walt Hanford, thirty years younger, shrugged thick shoulders. "Cattle're better, Sam. Cattle are the future of the West. Buffaloes was just an interlude."

Sloan sucked his pipe, gazing at the saloonman. "So are we, maybe."

After old Sam had departed, three bearded freighters arrived, and Walt Hanford forgot both old Sam and what he had said.

Andrew Cameron, whose huge ranch covered more country than a man could ride over in weeks, ventured out with one of his hired men, looking for a missing bull. He was somewhat older than Sam Sloan, but he'd

2

never killed a buffalo. He had brushed them aside as he had labored mightily to create an empire of deeded land and the cattle to stock it. It was rumored in Boulder that Cameron was wealthy. If he was, no information of that kind ever came from Andrew Cameron. He was a thin-lipped, weathered cowman with sunk-set gray eyes who spoke when he had something to say. Otherwise he listened.

While they were searching, the hired man suddenly stood in his stirrups. "Who in hell is that?" he exclaimed and pointed.

Cameron reined up, rested both hands atop the horn, and watched.

The other rider said: "He's walkin' toward the mountains . . . on foot, for Christ's sake."

Cameron said nothing. The mountains were distant, massive, and heavily timbered. As they resumed their search, the hired man tried to keep the topic of the walker alive but let it die because his companion would not be drawn out.

They didn't find the bull. With dusk coming, they turned back toward the home place, a sprawl of log structures, shaded in summer by cottonwoods the old man had planted years back. Andrew Cameron kept three rangemen through the summer, only one through the winter. They lived in a log bunkhouse, while their employer lived in a larger log house at the most southern end of the yard. As far as anyone knew, Andrew Cameron had never married. His existence for the past thirty years had been dedicated to his cow outfit.

Once a month the county sheriff, a stolid, soft-spoken man, Walt Hanford, and a man named Turk Greenoff rode out for a poker session. As far as folks knew, that was Andrew Cameron's only diversion. Turk Greenoff was Boulder's wheelwright and blacksmith. He was dark, quiet, massively muscled, and had a sly sense of humor. They were not actually very different. None of them "blew smoke." None of them talked a lot. All of them played canny poker, and everyone of them had a streak of humor.

When the game was over, and John Finley, the sheriff, pocketed his winnings, Cameron set bottled Scotch on the table beside a box of cigars and addressed the lawman. "You know an old highbinder named Sloan?"

Sheriff Finley waved smoke away before answering. "I've known him eight or ten years. Why?"

"Me'n a rider was out lookin' for a missin' bull, and there he was, on foot, walkin' toward the mountains."

Sheriff Finley never shot from the hip, and he didn't this time. After a moment of silence he leaned to tip his little glass full as he said: "He lives in one of them tarpaper shacks at the lower end of town. Summertimes he raises one hell of a vegetable garden, sells things around town." Finley tipped ash before continuing. "He was a buffalo hunter. He told me one time he knew Cody an' Three-Finger Jack Koehler." The sheriff squinted at Cameron. "Walkin' toward the mountains? You sure it was him?"

Cameron nodded. "I'm sure. I've seen him around town for years. Why would he be doin' that, I wonder?"

4

Neither the sheriff nor the others could answer, but the wheelwright made a guess. "Goin' pot huntin' to sell meat around town?"

Cameron shook his head. "Not without a pack horse."

Sheriff Finley was on the porch, putting on his hat, when he told Cameron he'd hunt up Sloan in the morning.

A rangeman by the name of Luc — he pronounced it the same as Luke — had stayed for four consecutive years to work on the Cameron place. Luc Pernell found the missing bull two days later. It was by itself at a sump spring. It was too sore-footed to be driven, so Luc left it there.

As he and his boss were discussing this, Luc briefly strayed from the bull to say that, while he was at the sump spring in the foothills, he heard someone farther up, chopping wood. He waited for Cameron to growl. He did not like trespassers. But Cameron peered at some corralled horses and said nothing.

At the bunkhouse Luc told the other riders what he had heard. One man, bearded like a pard, built like a bear and who walked like one, said what the others were thinking. "The old man'll be all over that feller like a rash."

The following morning Cameron's big sorrel horse was gone. The rigging was not on the saddle pole at the barn, and the bear-like shaggy man made a wolfish grin. "That wood chopper's goin' to think the sky fell on him."

There was always work to be done. The Cameron riders, seasoned rangemen, did not have to be told what to do. They rode out with the rising sun and did not return until near dusk. This day, when they did, the old man's sorrel horse was not in the corral.

Luc shook his head. "Someone should've gone with him."

No one agreed or disagreed. They were tired and hungry. Over supper they speculated about what the old man might have encountered. The northerly mountains were miles deep, rugged and gloomy, and were known to have bears, cougars, and wolves in their depths. No Cameron rider ever went any farther than the foothills. They'd never had reason to go it. Their job was livestock, the kind that lived off grass. Grass did not grow in the mountains except in rare parks. Over the years Cameron had lost cattle to predators, mostly wolves at calving time, but now and then a curious critter would venture into the mountainous, timber country. If they were found, it was usually buzzards who led riders to the carcass.

The following morning the sorrel horse was again in the corral. The old man's outfit was on the saddle pole, but he did not leave the house until close to noon, when the rangemen had been gone for hours.

After breakfast he sat in a rocker on the porch, fired up a pipe, and gazed pensively northward. He did not stir until he saw the riders coming, then went down to the barn to lean on a tie rack while they off-saddled. They accepted his reticence. It was as much a part of him as the shrewd pale eyes and the mop of coarse, gray hair.

They explained what they had done during his absence. They hoped through imitation they might encourage him to explain his absence. He didn't. He told them he'd take the light wagon to Boulder for supplies in the morning and left them standing, while he crossed to the main house.

The bear-like rider growled and headed for the bunkhouse. As they were rassling supper, he said: "I been ridin' for Mister Cameron three seasons, an' by Gawd I don't know him any better now'n I knew him the first summer."

Because curiosity was not self-sustaining, after they cleared the table, they played cards. As they were boxing the cards, Luc Pernell leaned far back from the table as he said: "If I'd caught me a trespasser an' killed him, I'd never say anythin'."

The bear-built man gazed at Luc. "He might have. That's the trouble. You can't figure what he'd do, or what he wouldn't do."

The men turned out ahead of sunrise as usual, and the big sorrel horse and its gear was gone again. They said little until Billy Grover, the bear-like man, made a suggestion. "Him ridin' into them mountains by hisself. For his own good I think we'd ought to sashay around up there."

Luc's response to that was curt. "He won't like it, us wet nursin' him."

They left the yard, following the freshest shod-horse tracks which posed no problem. Andrew Cameron rode a twelve-hundred-pound animal with hoofs like dinner plates. They were careful. From the forested uplands riders crossing open grassland would be as noticeable as warts on a man's hand. They took advantage of every *bosque* of trees, every north-south arroyo, and every jumble of house-size boulders.

They stopped at a water hole where cattle fled in every direction, tanked up their animals, considered the uplands and speculated about Cameron's course as well as his reason for going into the high country. Jed Carville, the rider who had first seen a man on foot hiking toward the mountains, felt uncomfortable the closer they got to the rugged and gloomy highlands. "He'll fire the bunch of us," he complained.

Someone said: "I was lookin' for work when I come here'n I'll be doin' the same when I leave here."

Carville resumed the trail with the others by leaving it up to his horse to follow. He concentrated hard on peering ahead for the old man's silhouette or for movement. He had a bad feeling about what they were doing.

Billy Grover abruptly yanked to a halt. The others piled up behind him. The bear-like man sat twisted in the saddle, pointing behind them down their back trail. Cameron on his big sorrel horse was slow-loping southward in the direction of the yard. He had left the highlands about a mile to the westward.

As they watched, expecting the old man to look in their direction, Billy Grover said: "Son of a bitch!" and sat gazing up into the highlands where sunlight rarely reached. There was no movement up there. Billy reined

8

around to follow the old man, but neither he nor his companions boosted their horses out of a walk.

When they reached the yard, there was smoke rising from the kitchen at the main house. After caring for their animals, they trudged to the bunkhouse. After the stove had been fired up and the hanging lamp lighted, Luc Pernell filled a cup with black Java at the stove as he dourly wagged his head in the direction of the others. "Whatever he's doin' is all right. We got plenty to do without spyin' on him. It's none of our business, anyway."

For five days Andrew Cameron rode with his rangemen. He did not mention his absences, and none of the riders asked. It was one of the known facts about Andrew Cameron that, excluding his monthly poker players, he neither encouraged nor sought friendships.

Walter Hanford had once said of Andrew Cameron that, him being a Scot, folks shouldn't expect anything different. The Scots were a private folk. Where Hanford had got that scrap of information, he never said, but those who had been in the saloon, when he had said it, left the saloon with a sense of enlightenment. Maybe Hanford had a head on his shoulders for a fact. His pronouncement had hit the nail squarely on the head. Henceforth, folks would be able to understand old Cameron better.

The third time Andrew Cameron left in the dark he took along a pack horse, and that created genuine bafflement among his riders. Had they been able to see the pack animal, had they been able to see some of the things being packed, their bafflement would only have deepened.

Their jobs were perfunctory. They'd been doing them for years, and, while an infrequent diversion occurred, such as a mammy cow with a hung-up calf or wolves stalking newborns, not for the calves but for the afterbirth, their work at most times amounted to sheer boredom. It was during those times that they'd sit in tree shade to discuss the seemingly secretive behavior of Andrew Cameron.

Billy Grover seemed particularly curious. He even suggested that possibly the old man had found some hold-out Indians or maybe a compatible squaw. The others scoffed. Jed Carville said there hadn't been any tomahawks in the country for years, that the Army had rounded up every bronco it could find, and had driven them onto reservations.

Billy lowered his head, little eyes spiteful when he rebutted Carville. "There's always Injuns around . . . like ghosts. Sneakin' in the mountains, spyin' on folks. Last time there was any in the Boulder country, it was scattered bands, hidin' out an' gettin' caught. Anyway, Mister Cameron's too old to fancy a squaw."

"Then," Carville exclaimed, "what's he doin'? Billy, I've come back to ride for him as long as you have. A man could set his watch, if he had one, by what the old man would do."

The discussion ended when Luc Pernell arose, dusted off, mightily stretched, and started for his horse. He said: "Let's get back."

10

On the southward ride Billy Grover eased up to ride stirrup-to-stirrup with Jed Carville. Jed ignored him until Billy leaned and half whispered a fresh thought. "Gold, Jed. He's found gold back in there. I figger he's takin' diggin' tools and whatnot with him."

Carville considered the big man testily. He was still stung by their disagreement back yonder. "What in hell are you talkin' about? The old man's got more money than you could count. Why would he go pawin' around for gold?"

Billy straightened in the saddle, looking smug. "Partner, you ever heard of a feller named Crœsus?"

"No. Cowman?"

"He was the richest man in the world, but he never stopped tryin' to get richer."

Jed eyed his riding companion. "Who the hell is . . . ?"

"I heard a preacher in Arkansas tell about him."

"Was he an Arkansan? I never heard of a rich Arkansan."

"He's a feller who lived long ago, the preacher said."

Carville's disgust was mounting. "What's this Crœsus got to do with Mister Cameron?"

"Same thing. They both got plenty of money but want more."

Jed Carville urged his horse ahead until he was riding stirrup-to-stirrup with Luc Pernell. Luc considered the dour expression on Carville's face and wisely kept silent. Not until they had the yard in sight did Jed drift back where the bear-like man was slouching along. He did not look at Billy when he said: "Is there gold in them mountains?"

Grover brightened. "Sure as I'm settin' here. Ask around town, folks'll tell you there used to be dirt miners up in there."

Jed rode the rest of the distance to the yard without saying a word, nor did he speak while they were off-saddling and caring for their animals. Only when they were at supper did he bring up the old man's absences. He said: "Mister Cameron's bein' furtive, like he don't want anyone to know what he's doin' up in there."

No one offered to keep this topic alive. They had been jawing this subject for several weeks, and nothing new had come up. Billy Glover did not even look up when Jed spoke, so, while his curiosity may have lingered, perhaps his interest was also beginning to wane. After all, directly now it would be roundup time and that would fully occupy them.

CHAPTER
TWO

Sam's Meadow

Sam Sloan hadn't been young in quite a spell, had no idea who his parents were or when he had been born. An itinerant tooth-puller had once treated Sam and told him he had to be in his fifties. He'd added a year each time folks shot off guns when a new year came around. By his lights he was seventy-four when he left Boulder, walking toward the mountains.

He was about six feet tall, as sinewy as old rawhide, observant, thoughtful, and alone. He had been a dead shot during his days of buffalo hunting, and, although he had taken his rifle and an old Army six-shooter with him when he'd left town, he had fired neither in years.

He entered the mountains, rested on a ridge, looking back. If someone had asked Sam what he was doing and why, he could not have answered them to save his soul. He'd never liked towns, but that wasn't it. Before bedding down that first night, he had made a little dry-wood fire, parched some corn, drank creek water, and sat with his back to black silence to perform a rite he'd seen Indians perform. He cut off a snippet of coarse gray hair, put it to burn in his fire ring, and closed his eyes. But as the smoke rose no vision came.

Come dawn's light, he stirred the embers for a flame, parched another few handfuls of corn, tanked up again at the creek, and studied the lifts and fallows of the mountains, things he understood and with which he was comfortable. When the sun arrived, he left the cold ashes behind, hiking northward and a tad westerly. He knew what he was looking for, and found it — a place where the timbered uplands had a break below the serrated rims, what folks called a park and eventually would call a *meadow*.

He remained in the final fringe of trees for a full hour, studying the expanse of this flat timberless grassy place where a busy cold-water creek ran from the northeast to the southwest. A heavy doe was stirring and pawing to make a birthing bed. She did not see the mountain lion, but Sam did. The doe's full attention was on what she was about to do. When she'd got the birthing place to her satisfaction, she folded her legs and went down. Within moments the straining began. When the doe went down, the cougar began its stealthy stalk, staying low in tall grass.

Sam moved to a rough-barked old red fir tree, took a hand rest, waited until the cougar was ready to launch itself, and fired. The noise terrified the doe, but she could not spring up and flee. She bleated in terror. The cougar left the meadow in frantic leaps.

Sam methodically reloaded and sat with the rifle across his lap, watching the doe arise unsteadily to lick her fawn, occasionally throwing up her head to seek movement. It took another hour for the doe to nuzzle her baby into a wobbly retreat with her into the protection of the trees.

Sam walked the park. It was about thirty acres in size, roughly as wide as it was long. He hiked among the surrounding forest, studying trees of which many were huge, old, overripe mammoths which would have rotten cores. He walked the creek where his shadow sent trout scurrying. He caught four in an enclosed inlet, gathered dry twigs, and ate two, keeping two for breakfast.

He bedded down near the little fire and lay awake long enough to have a lengthy conversation with a bright blue star. This was how he had lived during his prime. The ground was warm. The world was still. He didn't awaken until the chill arrived. He fed twigs into the ashes, blew up a pencil-thin blaze, ate the remaining trout, and sat until the sun came over the highest tree tops. Then he hiked over the grassy place a second time. Whatever it was that had told him one night in his shack down in Boulder he should make what the broncos called a spirit quest had started his walk.

He had a double-bitted axe. He went among the trees, blazing ones he liked. It was springtime. He had until next autumn to make his house. The axe had a short handle. Not long or heavy enough to fell trees. He could fashion a longer handle. Searching for the right sapling for this, he ventured deeper into the timber and encountered a brown bear, slick and in its prime. His rifle was back with his blanket. The bear was as surprised as Sam was and had possibly never before seen another creature that could walk upright. It showed no fear, just curiosity.

Sam talked to it. "You'd make good eatin', but there'd be a lot of waste, so you go on an' someday we might meet again."

The bear hadn't moved. It wrinkled its face, tilted its head, and blew its nose before it sidled from sight among the trees, never taking its eyes off the upright two-legged being. Sam gave it plenty of time, even altered his course as he cruised the timber. He blazed a number of trees, mostly of a uniform size, and returned to the creek to catch supper and breakfast.

The following morning there were deer in the meadow. They were wary, but Sam ignored them to fry more trout. His back was to them, so he was unaware of their abrupt stance, poised for flight. Only when a four-point buck whistled did he look up and around. The deer showed white flags as they raced for the timber.

Sam ate trout, wiped his hands in the grass, and sat watching and listening. He saw what had frightened the deer before he heard it, a horseman picking his way in and out among the trees. Sam put his sidearm in his lap but otherwise did not move. He couldn't make the man out very well, but the horse was a big sorrel.

The rider saw Sam out in the meadow, reined to a stop, and sat a while, just looking. Eventually he rode out of the trees. He had a hard face, sunk-set eyes, a thatch as gray as Sam's hair, and had a Winchester in a saddle boot as well as a shell-belted Colt around his middle.

He was not smiling. Sam could sense the hostility before the horseman got near enough to halt for the second time, considering the dying fire, Sam's gatherings scattered close, and finally Sam himself. He said: "What's your name!"

"Sam Sloan. What's yours?"

"Andrew Cameron. What you doin' up here?"

That was harder to answer. While Sam hung fire, the other older man got stiffly down and trickled one rein through gnarled large fingers. Sam said: "Care for a fish?"

Andrew Cameron did not respond. He made another inspection of Sam and his gatherings, went the length of his rein, and squatted. "You know who owns this land, Mister Sloan?"

"No, sir, I surely don't."

"I heard you choppin' wood."

"Blazin' trees for a cabin. Are you Andrew Cameron who ranches south of here?"

"Yep." Cameron's unwavering stare did not leave Sam. "A cabin?"

Sam's gaze went to the big sorrel horse and back. "Mind if I tell you somethin', Mister Cameron?"

He got no answer from the grizzled cowman.

"You believe in spirits, Mister Cameron?"

For the second time Sam got no answer, just a baleful stare.

"I been a trapper, a scout an' a buffler hunter." Sam made a slight gesture with his hands. "Folks quit wearin' beaver hats fifteen years ago. Scoutin' paid seven dollars a month, then the Army corralled the

Injuns. The buffler are gone, an' by my calculations I'm better'n seventy years old. Injuns had spirits. They talked to stars. I got a powerful urge to go and find a spirit place. Don't make sense, does it?"

Cameron broke his silence. "You walked up here?"

"I ain't owned a horse in fifteen years."

Cameron hunkered, studied Sloan's gatherings, fished out his pipe, stuffed it with shag, and was about to light it when he saw the way Sloan was watching. He fished out his pouch and tossed it over. They both fired up off the same sputtering lucifer.

Cameron remained quiet for a long time, and Sam Sloan made no attempt to break the silence. The sorrel horse nickered. Sam unwound up off the ground as he said: "I'll water him."

Cameron watched as his big sorrel was led to the creek. His eyes barely flickered when Sloan removed the bridle before allowing the animal to drink. He made another study of Sloan's gatherings, particularly of the rifle with its bird's eye maple stock. He hadn't seen a weapon like that in a very long time.

As Sam returned with the horse, Cameron said: "Set," and offered a lucifer for Sam to relight his pipe. "Where do you figure to put that cabin?"

Sam gestured. "Near the creek but northerly, closer to the trees."

Cameron removed his pipe. "I knew a feller up in Wyoming name of Shipman. He put his house right up next to the trees, an' the followin' summer we found him so full of arrers he looked like a pincushion."

Sam nodded. "How long ago was that?"

"Fifteen, twenty years."

"Injuns been pretty scarce since then, Mister Cameron."

The cowman ignored that to ask a question. "You got the trees blazed?"

"As many as I'll need to get started."

"An' how're you goin' to drag them down where you figure to make the cabin?"

"Well, draw-knife 'em where they fall, then roll 'em."

Andrew Cameron made a slight snorting sound. "How old did you say you was?"

"Seventy somethin', but I can do it. A man can do just about anythin' if he's got to."

"Where you from?" Cameron asked.

"Just about everywhere. I got no idea where I was born nor who my folks was. I been quite a few years in northern New Mexico. I lived down at Boulder the last of them years."

Andrew Cameron arose, flinched when a knee briefly cramped, went to his horse, snugged up the cinch, and mounted. He evened up his reins, then sat a moment, gazing at Sam Sloan before he fished out his tobacco sack, tossed it, and without another word reined back the way he had come.

Cameron returned several days later with a heavy, long-handled broad-bitted axe and a draw-knife. He hobbled his horse to graze and ate some tinned peaches he had brought. Sam did not appear until late afternoon. He saw the horse first, then the grizzled cowman, and called a greeting which Cameron did not return, but he almost imperceptibly nodded.

"Been huntin'," Sam Sloan said.

Cameron had a dry remark to make about that. "Yonder's a new axe an' a draw-knife. You can hunt any time. Gettin' logs down comes first. There's a tin of peaches an' some tobacco in that croaker sack."

Sam considered the sack and faced around as Cameron came up off the ground.

"Let's make some wood," Cameron said and went after his horse.

Sam waited, watched, wondered. He'd heard of Andrew Cameron, and evidently what he'd heard was right. Andrew Cameron was a blunt, dogged, and no-nonsense individual. That much Sam Sloan was ready to believe. He went over to thank the cowman for what he'd brought.

Cameron turned his back, swung over leather, and jutted his jaw. "Fetch the axe."

The day was warm and waning. They went north where Sam felled four trees. During a rest, Cameron said: "You marked out where the house is goin' to be?"

"You rode past it. Them stakes drove in the ground."

Cameron squinted southward, opened a saddlebag, and tossed a light length of chain to the ground. "Two half hitches," he ordered. "At the big end."

They dragged the four downed trees to the cabin site. Cameron's pudding-footed big sorrel horse had no difficulty. Sam marveled. He'd owned many horses, not always as large as the sorrel, but he'd never owned one

20

that could snake logs, and Cameron did it all from the saddle with the light chain double-dallied.

When they had the last log in place, Cameron dismounted, loosened the cinch, removed the bridle, and hobbled his horse.

He stepped off the distance between stakes and pursed his mouth. "Good sized cabin. I started out with one half as big. Draw-knife 'em. The horse can rest a spell, then I got to get back."

Sam's idea had been to strip the bark where he felled the trees. After Cameron left, he cut the logs to length and draw-knifed every bit of bark off. It went well because in springtime there is moisture under the bark. He finished by moonlight, moved his camp closer to where the cabin would be, ate jerky and tinned peaches, and bedded down. Wolves scouted him up in the dark. He listened to them and smiled. Sleep came and so did chilly dawn. He rolled out, ate what he had left from last night, and worked until the sun was overhead. Then he went to the creek to take an all-over bath and sit in the grass until he was dry.

He thought of two things — his house and old Cameron. He went fishing in the afternoon to lay by supper and another breakfast. Just short of sundown he took the rifle and hunted, but, if there had been game, his appearance, noise, and alien scent had cleared the area. He found no meat, but he came across something nearly as good: a bee tree.

Because bears routinely tore the heart out of bee trees for the honey, some hives would not den up less than ten to twenty feet from the ground. This nest was a good fifteen feet up in a rough-barked old forest mammoth. He might have missed it except for the busy buzzing. He circled the tree, watched hordes of bees enter a hole and emerge, saw where the inner storing had slightly darkened the bark, and decided to come back in broad daylight.

But not the next day because the powerful sorrel horse and its rider appeared leading a pack mule. Sam learned a little more about Andrew Cameron. After they had unloaded the mule, hobbled both animals in tall grass, and began emptying the *alforjas*, Sam gazed from the mound of supplies to the man who had brought them.

"I got no money, Mister Cameron."

The cowman's retort was brusque. "I didn't ask for none."

"But . . ."

"Get the axe. We got logs to haul."

"Mister Cameron . . . ?"

The grizzled stockman turned on Sam. "I don't want to hear no more about it. Get the axe!"

They put in a long day. The pile of logs grew, and this time they ate together.

Cameron said: "Keep the chain. Before you get an animal, you got to have a scythe. Winters up here is long an' hard." He chewed and considered the meadow. "You can cut five, six tons of hay when you're restin'."

This time, after the cowman left, Sam Sloan sat on a draw-knifed log, looking at the tins and tools, and shook his head. He hadn't expected help, wouldn't have asked for it, and did not like the idea of being beholden.

When the sorrel horse did not appear the following day, Sam returned to the bee tree with some rope, a hand axe, and a wad of dry grass tied to the end of a stick. He couldn't smoke the bees out from the ground. The hole was too high. In anticipation of that he used the rope to lariat a thick limb and to climb with the dry-grass stick stuck in the back of his britches.

It was arduous work. The bees did not like him being close. He was stung, but mostly the bees flew a zigzag course around his face and shoulders, which was their way of warning him off. He was high enough to secure the rope, so he could use both hands to fire the dry grass and smoke them out, when a sound below turned him rigid and motionless.

Generations of pine and fir needles not only made spongy earth cover, they also muffled sound, but what Sam heard was approaching movement accompanied by something or someone using a stick to knock low branches aside. Bears blundered through, but their noise was different. And bears commonly whined, groaned, and talked to themselves as they traveled.

It was gloomy in the forest. In rare places, where sunshine came through, ancient dust was in the light. Where Sam had become part of his tree, there was no sunlight.

The tapping stick stopped. Sam felt for his belt gun. If he had been seen up here, hugging a tree, he would make an easy target. The bees still circled but in fewer numbers, and they no longer attacked. Sam could place the direction of the tapping. It was east of him, coming in his direction.

When the tapping was very close, Sam saw the tapper, a scrawny Indian using the stick with his left hand and carrying an old Army issue Sharps carbine in the other hand. The bronco's hair was awry, his clothing stained and worn. On his belt he had a stag-handled fleshing knife and an old hawgleg holstered six-gun. He also carried a small leather pouch.

He stopped a foot or two past the bee tree. He had heard the buzzing. Sam turned loose all holds and dropped like a plummet. The Indian had seconds to react to a man, dropping on him from the treetop, and didn't. He grunted as Sam slammed into him, taking them both to the ground.

The bronco tried to get his big knife. Sam struck him alongside the jaw with one hand and blocked his knife hand with the other arm. The Indian was stunned, but he struggled until Sam, with better aim, knocked him senseless.

For a long moment Sam continued to straddle the Indian. When he eventually arose, he sucked air, disarmed the unconscious man, and stood looking down. The Indian's clothing was not quite ragged, but his moccasins were almost worn through. The little pouch he wore had once been decorated with an elegant design made of flattened porcupine quills. Sam leaned to yank a chain barely visible around the Indian's neck. It held a small silver oblong religious medal.

Sam looked up. The bees were back, going and coming. They paid no attention to the men on the ground.

Sam emptied the charges from the Indian's weapons, and, when their owner groaned, rolled over, and scrabbled in the ground to arise, Sam grabbed him by the neck and yanked him upright. The Indian's dark eyes had muddy whites. His skin was lined and weathered. He hadn't been young in many years.

He made a tentative smile. Sam held him by the collar, shoved him away, and herded him to the log pile where the Indian sat down, looking at the ground. Sam dumped the emptied weapons and said: "You old son of a bitch, what you doin' up here?"

"Hunt."

Sam was disgusted. "Hittin' trees with a stick? Every critter for half a mile could hear you. What kind of Injun are you?"

"Hungry," the Indian said, eyeing Sam's supplies. "Much hungry." The eyes with their muddied whites went to Sam's face and remained there.

Sam gazed at the bronco in long silence. He was an old Indian, skinny as a snake and weak. Sam used the Indian's knife to open a tin of peaches and held it out. The Indian emptied the tin in moments, held it in his lap, making his forlorn little smile again. When Sam reached for the empty tin can, the old Indian gripped it, would not release it.

Sam sat on a log. "You got a camp up in here?"

"No. Many days hunting. Go long ways around towns."

25

"You got a name?"

"Steals-Many-Horses."

Sam gazed over where the stakes indicated his house would be. If Cameron came up here again, as he surely would do, and met an Indian whose name meant he had been a successful horse thief . . . Sam said: "You go now."

Steals-Many-Horses was gazing at the mound of supplies when he replied. "I stay."

Sam scowled. "You go!"

"You make *hogan?* I help." He jutted his chin in the direction of the supplies. "You pay with food."

Sam watched the old man's toes scuff dust through his moccasins. Sam had been around Indians most of his life. He had figured out what kind of bronco the old man was by his moccasins with their three silver buttons, his lack of beadwork, and the lack of feathers.

"Strong," the Indian said, and Sam ruefully nodded. Steals-Many-Horses was weak as a kitten. Sam should know. He had pinned the old man to the ground with no effort. He told the Indian he did not need help and saw the look in the dark eyes with muddied whites. Sam knew what hunger and destitution were. He had experienced them both many times. Nothing broke the human spirit the way they did.

He told the Indian to fetch water from the creek, and they'd have supper. Steals-Many-Horses went dutifully toward the creek, clutching his empty peaches can.

Sam called. "Take the bucket!"

The Indian dutifully got the bucket in one hand and gripped his empty peaches can in the other. Sam sat watching. The Indian was starving. Well, maybe he could use him. Four hands were better than two. Conversely, Sam Sloan wanted this to be his personal undertaking. He needed a starved old Indian like he needed a busted leg.

CHAPTER
THREE

One From The South, Now One From The East

Steals-Many-Horses tired easily, which Sam made a point of not noticing. But, for a fact, the old bronco knew something about squaring and notching logs to fit. Sam told him not to be so damned finicky about the fit. They'd chink the walls with mud. Steals-Many-Horses smiled — and continued to draw-knife the logs so that they fit like gloves.

They devised a lift the closer they got to the final logs. Cameron's chain made this possible. A block and tackle would have been better, but, since they had none, they had to use old backs and muscles. Steals-Many-Horses sat for long periods between the hoisting, but, as days passed, he sat less often and for shorter periods of time.

His moccasins gave out. He acted embarrassed about this and worked barefoot. They had the walls in place and for the ensuing two days hunted. They returned to the bee tree, where Steals-Many-Horses considered

Sam's rope sling as he said: "I go up. You hand me stick with grass."

Sam shook his head. "You hand up the stick," and went to the sling. Steals-Many-Horses waited until Sam was ready to climb, told him to light the torch first, which Sam did not do, and was attacked again, this time from all directions by angry bees. He had to descend, bees following him all the way. Steals-Many-Horses dug for moist earth, handed fistfuls to Sam, took the stick, and started to climb. Midway he fired a lucifer and applied it to the dry grass. The thing burned like a torch, giving off a whitish smoke until Sam could not see either the bee hole or Steals-Many-Horses.

Sam said: "Stuff it in the hole," which the Indian did but not until dazed and dying bees fell around Sam like rain. When the hole was plugged, the Indian climbed down. He had been stung three times.

On the hike back to the meadow he told Sam they shouldn't cut the tree down until they had a place to store honey, and Sam scowled. They wouldn't have a storeroom shed until autumn, if then.

They went to the creek to soothe their stings. Steals-Many-Horses was slathering cold watery mud when he said: "Horse coming."

He was right, but the big sorrel horse did not appear for another fifteen minutes, by which time Sam and his helper were over in front of the cabin where they had made a bench and two chairs. Green fir ran sap. Neither of them used the chairs, and they had covered the seat of the bench with a layer of fir needles.

Andrew Cameron stopped when past the final stand of trees. Sam smiled without speaking. As the cowman continued toward the cabin, his expression did not change. He dismounted, looked around, and finally spoke. "Where's the damned tie rack?" and stared at Steals-Many-Horses. "Where'd he come from?"

Steals-Many-Horses made his sad little diffident smile, took the reins, and led the horse out to grass to be hobbled. Old Cameron watched everything the Indian did, and Sam Sloan squirmed. That big sorrel horse was an animal a horse thief might encounter no more than ten times in his career.

Cameron faced Sam. "Well . . . ?"

"I found him so starved he could hardly walk. He helps around."

Cameron looked out where the Indian was admiring the grazing sorrel horse. "Speak English? He's older'n dirt."

"Speaks passable English."

Cameron moved to one of the chairs, eyed the seat, and went to the bench. "One of them border-cross Navajos? Where's his moccasins?"

"Wore through."

"Got three silver buttons, have they?"

"Yes. Old ones."

Cameron nodded. "They pass 'em down from father to son." He eyed the bench as he had the chairs, eased down gently, and groped for his pipe. "You got the walls up." He fired up the pipe before continuing. "The tomahawk help?"

"He helped. He fit the logs so's you can hardly get a knife blade between 'em."

Trickling smoke and gazing out where the Indian was, Cameron said: "I liked 'em wild. Tame ones'll steal an axe before the haft is cool."

He offered Sam his pouch. Sam filled his pipe with his own tobacco. "You never saw such a measly person as he was."

"Yes I have. Plenty times. When they was free, they was different. They could steal a horse right out from under you, an' they run off cattle, traded them over the line to Messicans. In those days you knew 'em. Nowadays . . . ? What's his name?"

Sam waited until he had a head of smoke rising before answering. "Many-Horses."

Cameron nodded flintily. "I expect so. What're you goin' to do with him?"

Sam watched Steals-Many-Horses, leaving the sorrel horse as he hiked toward the cabin. "I don't know."

"You better get rid of him. One of these mornings you'll wake up with nothing but your britches."

Sam arose. "Come inside."

Cameron stood in the middle of the big room. Once he went to a wall and felt where one log was atop the other. He went to the far wall and tapped it. "Put a window here. Skulkers'll come on your blind side." He looked up at the summer sky. "You got rafters cut?"

"Yes."

Cameron stood in the doorway. "Damned Injun's disappeared."

They went over to the fire ring where Sam scuffed for coals to make a fire. Cameron watched and said: "A man can eat anytime. He can only work durin' daylight."

They returned to the bench at the front of the cabin where Cameron sat gingerly and refired his pipe. When he had a head of smoke, he asked if Sam had enough rafters cut.

"Enough, and draw-knifed up where we work."

Cameron shifted on the bench. "Where's that damned Injun? I don't like 'em behind me."

Sam learned something about the grizzled cowman. He did not like Indians, which was not unusual. Most folks didn't like Indians.

Cameron arose, flexed one knee. "I'll take the horse up yonder. Is the chain up there?"

As soon as the cowman started away from the cabin, Steals-Many-Horses came around the east side of the house. "*Viejo* don't like Injuns."

"*¿Viejo?* His name's Andrew Cameron."

"*Viejo* means old one. He don't want me to stay."

Sam stood up. "I'm beholden to him, but I found this park, and he don't tell me who stays an' who don't."

Steals-Many-Horses stood his ground when the grizzled cowman led his horse back to be saddled and bridled. They exchanged one look before Cameron turned his back.

They went north to the log landing. Steals-Many-Horses made the pair of hitches on the first log and stepped back. As Cameron eased ahead to take up slack, the chain came loose. He looked back as he said: "Dumb bastard. Do it right."

Steals-Many-Horses did it right. He cast three half hitches this time. The big sorrel horse leaned into the weight as though he'd been dragging logs all his life.

They worked until nearly sundown, getting nearly all the logs down to the cabin. Cameron took his horse to the creek, tanked it up, removed the saddle, and, using swatches of moist grass, washed its back. Sam smiled.

When Andrew Cameron left, Steals-Many-Horses watched him pass from sight among the trees, went out to the creek to sluice off, and returned with dry twigs for the supper fire. Every time he had a chance, he gathered kindling. There was a respectable pile of it on the cabin's lee side.

Sam Sloan did not say much until they'd finished eating and dusk was settling. He was troubled by the cowman's obvious antipathy toward Steals-Many-Horses. The old bronco learned quickly and anticipated things. Sam had come to depend on him. If Mr. Cameron didn't want him in Sloan's big meadow . . . For a fact, he owed the cowman. Also, when he had started walking, his intention was to seek a private place — *Sam Sloan's place.*

The bronco's solemn gaze with its muddy whites were fixed on Sam. As he wiped his fingers, he said: "I go."

Sam flared up. "You stay! Where would you go?"

"Just go."

Sam fished for his pipe. "That old cavalry carbine of yours couldn't hit the side of a barn from the inside.

Many-Horses, me'n you got somethin' in common. We're old." Sam made a gesture. "You go an' someday they'll find your shrunk-up carcass. Let's clean up here."

Steals-Many-Horses stood out in the dusk for a long time. Occasionally he looked northward where timber-covered miles ended against some ragged-tooth rims. This wasn't his country. He was a desert Indian. All the *Dineh* were desert people. In his father's day they had been uplands people, but the arrival of the white-eyes-all-dressed-the-same ended that. Steals-Many-Horses had known little else until the only link with his clan, his son, had died.

For two days he had sat alone in a place called Blue Cañon where what remained of Anasazi mud dwellings built under the overhang of a cliff were known among his people to be haunted. The third day he had taken what he needed and had started walking. He had been walking a long time — about a year. There had been times when he thought he was supposed to walk until he became too weak. Then he would die.

Where the desert people were held was close to the U.S.- Mexico border. In his youth no horse thief had excelled him. He had stolen horses in the night from the white-eyes, had sold or traded them to the Mexicans, had stolen from the Mexicans, and sold horses among his tribesmen, even the white traders. A whisper of moving grass brought him around.

Sam said: "Nice night."

"Yes."

34

"Tell me somethin', Many-Horses. How come you to speak English?"

"There was always traders, buyers. I grew up with their language. Like Mexicans, you be around them long enough, you learn." Many-Horses fished inside his old shirt. "Mexican priest give me this. It's a sacred medal. You see the saint on it? He protects me."

Sam leaned, squinted, and said: "Uhn-huh," and did not say what he thought — a saint that'd let an old man dang near starve to death most likely wasn't much of a protector.

Many-Horses regarded Sloan. "You knew this place?"

"No, never seen it before the day I walked up here."

"You had a home somewhere?"

"Well, lots of places. Lastly down at a town called Boulder." Sam shifted his weight and stood hip-shot. "Never liked towns, never much liked hunters' camps."

"So you found this place?"

"I expect you could say that. It come to me one day to find a place of my own."

"And you started walking?"

"Yep, just started walking."

Their discussion was abruptly interrupted by the sounds of a furious fight. What sounded like a cow or a bull was making slobbering bellows, and a cougar was snarling and spitting. Many-Horses said: "Get rifle," and started swiftly in the direction of the fight. Sam ran to the house, grabbed his rifle, and loped after the old Indian.

It wasn't really much of a fight. A filthy, shaggy old buffalo cow was down, trying to use her horns, mouth open, tongue curled inward as she bawled. The cougar was in his prime, big and powerful. He was on the old cow's back, claws deep, with blood flowing. He was trying to catch the old cow when she flung her head so he could tear her throat.

Many-Horses yelled something Sam did not understand and started toward the big cat with a drawn knife. Sam yelled at him. "Get out of the way, you old bastard!"

At the last moment, as the cougar looked up, Sam fired. The cat fell and threshed. Many-Horses sheathed his knife and ignored the cougar. When Sam came up, the Indian pointed to the claw marks and said: "Mud."

Sam stood looking at the large old animal whose ribs were visible beneath a shaggy lusterless coat of hair. The cow looked at the men. This time her defiant bawl was quavery. Many-Horses used his knife to dig for moist earth which he heaped on the bleeding claw marks.

Sam wrinkled his nose. He'd seen hundreds of buffalo, and none had ever had as foul a smell as this one. Many-Horses found the reason, when the cow tried to arise twice, and fell back. She had a running sore where a swollen rib showed. Many-Horses probed, poked, and squeezed until the steel bullet popped out.

Sam shook his head. Where pus had run there was no hair. It was an old wound. He pocketed the bullet and watched Many-Horses work over the old cow. She did not resist. She was past even trying to resist.

Sam brushed the Indian's shoulder. "I'll put her out of her misery," he said and was shocked at the old bronco's reaction.

Steals-Many-Horses turned, facing Sam, and flourished his knife. "No! You don't kill her!"

Sam grounded the rifle and leaned on it. "She's half dead, can't get up. She's starved down to bone. She's bled a lot. She's older'n dirt."

Many-Horses acted as though he had not heard. He got the cow's head raised, propped it with one leg to support it, and picked dirt from around her small eyes. "We take her to meadow," he said.

Sam rolled his eyes. "She can't get up, for Christ's sake."

Many-Horses did not look at Sam, "You got medicine bundle?"

Sam frowned and spoke as though to a child. "Listen to me, that old girl's on her last legs. She's too old to get through another winter. There's maggots in the bullet hole. More'n likely she's shed all her grinders."

Many-Horses still did not look up. "You get medicine box."

"Many-Horses, she's too old'n weak. It'd favor the old girl to shoot her."

This time, when the Indian looked up, his dark eyes with their muddy whites were uncompromising in their stare. "You go. I bring her!"

Sam said: "You crazy old bastard, she's gone her last mile. You ain't goin' to bring her nowhere. She can't even get up."

Sam turned on his heel, rifle in the fold of his right arm, and stamped disgustedly in the direction of the cabin.

Dusk had passed. Night was down. There was a huge moon which made visibility excellent. Sam reached the cabin, put the rifle aside, filled and lighted his pipe until little whitish puffs arose, and wondered for the hundredth time why he hadn't run off the old bronco when he'd first appeared. Taking off his boots, he climbed into his bunk and pulled up the covers.

Twice Sam sat up to look over where Many-Horses empty bunk was. The last time he raised up, it was to the sound of foraging wolves. He listened for a long time. They'd scented the old cow's blood. He flung back his bedding, stamped into his boots, grabbed his rifle on the way out, and soundly cursed Many-Horses.

All the bronco had been carrying when they'd found the cow had been his fleshing knife, and wolves were not particular when they followed blood-scent to living creatures. To wolves on a blood-scent, how many legs prey had made no difference.

Midway across the meadow Sam stopped in mid-lope. The buffalo cow was eating grass. She paused briefly to study Sam, then went back to eating.

He did something he normally did not do. He waited until he placed the sound of wolves and fired in that direction. The old cow had to be deaf. She did not even raise her head, but the retreating wolves were traceable by the direction and diminishing sound of their baying and howling.

Many-Horses was mounded under his blankets when Sam got back and leaned his rifle aside. His long drawers were wet from dew. He glared, got back under his covers, and could not come down from his exasperation for a good half hour.

In the morning Many-Horses was preparing a meal when Sam came out. Many-Horses's smile was that of an eight-year-old youngster. He jutted his jaw. "Coffee hot."

Sam sat, ignored the coffee whose aroma was tempting, and said: "How'd you get her on her feet?"

"She got up. I lean on one side. She come one step, two step."

Sam looked out where the old cow was grazing, filled a tin cup, and after one sip put the cup aside. The coffee was hot enough to blister the *cajones* off an iron monkey.

Three birds landed on the old cow's back. She ignored them. Lice pickers had been landing on her since she had been a calf.

After they had eaten, they worried several rafters aloft. Many-Horses had the agility of a simian. He was balancing up there when he told Sam they should run a center ridgepole the full length; otherwise, when they spaced the rafters for spiking, some of the rafters would be farther from the others.

Sam digested this slowly. He had never built a house before, and it required no experience to put up the walls. As he pondered, Many-Horses got precariously between two rafters and demonstrated that with a ridgepole in place they could use splayed fingers to assure each rafter was properly located in relation to the others.

Sam watched the Indian get back to safety and nodded his head. They put uprights at each end of the roof, spiked them, then levered and muscled and grunted the ridgepole up until it rested atop the uprights at both ends. Many-Horses spiked, and Sam stood down below, squinting. He asked if the pole was straight, and this time the old bronco climbed down, got an empty bottle, filled it with water, and climbed back up. As Sam watched, the Indian shook his head. "Too high in the middle." He held up the bottle. "Big bubble inside. Bubble has to be in middle."

He climbed down as someone hailed them from the timber. It was Andrew Cameron, and this time he was riding a stud-necked, seal-brown horse. He rode up, studied the ridgepole, and dismounted.

Many-Horses went to take the horse to the creek. As the old cowman watched, he said: "He'll take root, and you'll never get shed of him."

Sam got the bottle with the bubble, showed it to Cameron, and explained how they had made certain the ridgepole was straight. As Cameron took the bottle, Sam said: "That was his doings."

Cameron handed back the bottle. "They're like mules. You can't teach 'em a damned thing, but they can watch you do somethin' an' do the same thing tomorrow."

They went inside where the cowman looked up for a long time.

"You got a steep pitch. That's good. In this country anythin' with less of a pitch, when three foot of snow settles on the roof, it'll fall in." He eyed Sam. "Where'd that old buffalo cow come from?"

Sloan explained about the fight while Cameron said nothing. Not until they were outside, where the grazing cow was broadside to them, did he speak. "Must've been quite a fight. She got tore up pretty bad. Where'd she come from?"

Sam had no idea. "She was in the timber on the west side of the park."

"Hoofs wore down, are they?"

Sam hadn't examined her feet. His delay in answering prompted the cowman to say: "She's been walkin' a long time." He fished for his pipe. "That's an old buffalo. See that long belly hair under her? She's wormy." Cameron got the pipe lighted. "Old, weak, sick with worms, most likely her grinders are gone. Damned wonder she come through the mountains, an' wolves didn't drag her down."

Many-Horses came around the side of the cabin, smiling. Cameron eyed him through fragrant smoke and said: "Navajo?" pronouncing it as Mexicans did, Nav-*ah*-ho.

Many-Horses's smile broadened. "*Sí.*"

"*¿Habla . . . ? ¿Catolica?*"

This time Many-Horses gave a delayed response, in English. "Baptized *Catolica*," and shrugged.

Cameron's pipe went out. As though Many-Horses was not standing there, he addressed Sam. "They catch 'em young, Messican sisters, nuns." He looked squarely at Many-Horses. "With them, it's like paintin' a fence. You cover what's underneath, but what's under there stays." He nodded at the partially visible chain around the Indian's neck. "¿Catolica medalla?"

"Sí. Yes, Sainted Guadalupe." Many-Horses came closer and jutted his jaw. "You?"

Sam had never noticed what little was visible around the cowman's neck. Cameron's gaze showed faint irony as he nodded before answering in Spanish. "Sí, érase que se era." Yes, but not good at it.

Many-Horses laughed. "Me too."

"But you wear the medal."

"Navajo belief never helped. I wear medal, but it don't help, too. Maybe some day. ¿Quién sabe?"

Cameron fired up his pipe again while eyeing the Indian. He said: "Cover all bets. Me, too. What you goin' to do with that old buffalo cow?"

"Make her well."

"She's too old."

Many-Horses did not smile at Cameron, but there was a hint of something close to humor in his eyes when he said: "Me too old. Sam too old. You too old."

Andrew Cameron's flinty gaze went out where the cow was now lying down, belly full, dozing. Again his pipe went out. He continued to gaze out there when he addressed Sam. "You know how to split sugar pine shakes for the roof?"

Sam shook his head, no.

As the cowman arose, flexing his troublesome leg, he said: "This one knows," and went out to get his horse.

Sam looked at Many-Horses. "What'n hell is a sugar pine shake?"

"For roof. Keeps out water."

"You know how to make 'em?"

"Yes."

Sam returned to watching Cameron who was leading his horse back to be rigged out. Many-Horses spoke quietly: "He don't like Injuns."

Sam's reply was slowly given. "I wouldn't bet money on that. How come you speak Mexican?"

"Mission. They talked Mexican and English. I learned both."

"How long was you at the mission?"

"Eleven years."

Sam wanted to ask why Many-Horses had left, but the cowman, leading his horse, was too close.

Cameron rigged out and mounted. For a long moment he looked down, then barely nodded at Sam Sloan, started to rein away, and looked at Many-Horses. He did not nod. He winked.

There was not much daylight left, but they went back to working on the rafters, saying very little and then only about what they were doing.

That night Sam gazed past the skeleton-like poles overhead at the enormous gaggle of stars. He'd known his share of tomahawks without ever knowing one whose knowledge was as extensive as the knowledge of Steals-Many-Horses. He fell asleep more convinced than ever that regardless of what Andrew Cameron or anyone said, he was going to keep the Indian.

CHAPTER
FOUR

From The North

It required a particular tree for roof shakes, and sugar pines rarely grew at high elevations. Neither did oaks. High country timber was predominately fir. Many-Horses mumbled something about cedars — heart wood from burnt cedars — making the best shakes. Sam Sloan hadn't seen a cedar in years. They searched for hours. Many-Horses was not hopeful but kept this to himself.

They went farther than either of them had gone before and found where the meadow creek came from higher up through a rocky place. They rested, ate, drank cold water, and Many-Horses stiffened on all fours at the creek, dripping water. After a moment he held up a hand for Sam to be still. They were in a gloomy place of huge trees whose stiff tops kept the sun out.

Many-Horses stood up. Leaving his carbine with Sam, he blended into shadows. Hair on the back of Sam's neck stood up. He narrowed his eyes to study the area. Whatever had spooked Many-Horses did not appear, nor was there any sound. He leaned the Sharps gun aside, held his own rifle in his lap, thumb on the hammer, finger curled inside the trigger guard.

When Many-Horses returned, he came from the north, sat down, took back his carbine, and sat in silence until Sam said: "Well, you old bastard?"

"Tracks. Hard to read for tree needles. Don't make much deep."

"Where?"

Many-Horses jutted his jaw northward. "I lost 'em. They went to edge of creek, never come out other side." He looked at Sam. "Went in water."

"Which way?"

Many-Horses shook his head. "Don't know. You want to hunt for where they came out of creek?"

Sam considered the forest. It was miles in all directions. He said: "If it's a hostile, most likely he seen us."

Many-Horses agreed. "Maybe watch us now. We go back."

Sam straightened up. Everyone knew about holdouts, Indians who had either avoided being captured or were reservation jumpers. Horses disappeared from cow camps; weapons disappeared from bunkhouses after riders had ridden out.

When they started back, Sam hiked ahead. Many-Horses covered his back. He looked over his shoulder often. Something troubled him about the tracks, but it only passingly occupied his mind — what did was getting to the meadow alive.

When they reached the log landing, they rested in a long silence. Day was dying when they resumed the trail. Where they passed the bee tree, neither man looked up.

The buffalo cow watched them cross out of timber to open country. At the cabin Many-Horses leaned his carbine aside, took a pail of grease, and went out to doctor the cow. She did not so much as lower her head or make a threatening grumble.

Sam got kindling, coaxed a supper fire to life, and did not look across the meadow. Occasionally he would gaze northward.

While they were eating, Sam asked a question. "What kind of an Injun?"

Many-Horses's answer was given around a mouthful of food. "Don't know."

"One Injun?"

"One track to creek."

Sam was washing supper down with Black Joe when he said: "We got to find him before he finds us."

"He knows where we are."

Sam pondered that and agreed, without saying so. What he eventually said was: "We better take turns sleepin'."

Many-Horses was cleaning his tin plate with dry dirt when he nodded.

Later he went out to the cow, who was lying with legs curled, solemnly glancing in the direction of the cabin. She saw Many-Horses start out, regurgitated a fresh cud which she chewed in a sideways, grinding motion the same way cattle did.

Many-Horses examined the wounds. The biggest danger was blowflies. They would not land or lay eggs in grease. He talked to the cow, who continued to gaze in the direction of the house and chewed her cud. She was old, which no doubt had much to do with her acceptance of the two-legged things, and, while she was recovering, she remained weak. She had no expression unless it was resignation.

Without haste she swung her massive head northward, little eyes partially hidden in a mat of dark, curly hair fixed on something distant. Many-Horses eased belly-down in the grass. He had only his fleshing knife. The old hawgleg pistol and the carbine were at the house. He skylined in that direction, but, if Sam was outside, he was not moving.

The cow's gaze remained fixed. She did not move, not even when Many-Horses started crawling through tall grass in the direction of the cabin. When he reached the cabin, Sam hissed for him to watch northward, which Many-Horses did from the northeast side of the cabin.

Bears were not night hunters. Neither were cougars, but wolves were and shared with their coyote cousins a predilection for barking and howling as they coursed the darkness. There was not a sound.

Many-Horses got his belt gun and carbine. He knelt and remained motionless until Sam hissed from the southeast corner. Many-Horses went back where they palavered.

Many-Horses related the cow's reaction and thought it must have been a scent. In their prime buffalo had poor eyesight. As old as this cow was, he did not think she had seen anything. He thought they should use stealth among the big trees to locate what was in the vicinity of the path they had made dragging logs.

Sam said: "We wait. He's got to come out of the trees to reach the house. Let him come to us."

They sat and waited until dawn arrived. The cow arose to graze, her interest in whatever had been her earlier concern forgotten. Sam and Many-Horses went inside to have a cold breakfast.

While they were eating, Sam Sloan said: "The son of a bitch is out there. If we show ourselves in daylight . . ."

Many-Horses wiped his chin before replying. "Go find him."

Sam did not disagree. When Many-Horses suggested they cross to the easterly forest, which was close, and hunt northward, Sam buckled his gun belt in place, picked up his rifle, and led off.

They had to cross less than two hundred feet of open country to reach the trees. Sam positioned himself at the northeast corner where Many-Horses had been during the night, took a firm grip on a log, and rested his rifle across his forearm. When he was ready, he said: "Run for it," which Many-Horses did. Sam looked once. Many-Horses ran like a pigeon, his toes turned toward each other.

Nothing happened. When Many-Horses was in position, he whistled, and Sam ran. He had long, strong legs.

Nothing happened.

They parted but kept each other in sight, as they soundlessly moved among big trees. It normally required about half an hour to walk from the cabin to the trail leading to the landing. This time it took them more than an hour, and, when they could see the trail through the trees, there was nothing in sight. Many-Horses crept ahead almost to the path's edge, crouched, and moved a foot at a time. He halted, sank to one knee bracing himself with the old cavalry weapon, and remained that way a long time.

Sam's impatience made him move like a cougar until the Indian heard him, arose, moved back among the trees. When Sam arrived, the Indian pointed in the direction of their cabin.

Sam said: "How? We watched all night."

Many-Horses did not lower his arm, hoisted his carbine to the crook of one arm, and started back the way they had come. When he stopped beside a tree, Sam halted beside him. He said: "The cow ain't upset."

Many-Horses nodded, watching the house. Sam would have started forward, but Many-Horses threw out an arm. Sam growled. Many-Horses said: "I go around to west side, you go from east side."

Sam scowled. "You think he's inside? How'n hell could he do that? We watched all night."

Many-Horses raised his old carbine. "You wait. I whistle. We both jump into doorway." Before moving off, Many-Horses also said: "Don't shoot on sight. He not bad."

Sam spoke to himself as he watched the Indian move away. "Not bad? You crazy bastard, he stalked us all night."

Forests have birds. Sam heard none. He moved warily in the direction of the easterly log wall. Old Cameron had said they should make a window hole. By the time Sam was against the wall, he could make a death's-head smile. A window in any wall and they wouldn't be able to do what they were doing.

A night bird whistled.

Sam held his rifle in both hands as he sidled around to the front wall. Many-Horses was already there, on the west side of the doorless opening. They each cocked weapons and sprang into the doorway.

The Indian was as swift as a shadow, diving beneath one of the bunks built against opposite walls.

Sam said: "For Christ's sake!"

Many-Horses leaned aside his carbine, went inside, and dropped to the ground. The noise was as though two bob cats were fighting in a croaker sack. Many-Horses yanked back his arm and jumped up. He was bleeding.

Sam came up to lean and fire under the bunk.

Many-Horses said: "No shoot!" in the same tone of voice he'd used when Sam had wanted to put the old buffalo out of her misery.

Sam pulled back.

Many-Horses drew his big knife, got belly-down, and said: "You come out!" The answer he got was a furious rush of words with no pause between and a wide sweep by a claw-like hand, holding a knife. Many-Horses sat back and looked at Sam. "You know what he say?"

Sam hadn't any idea. He dropped down and peered beneath the bunk. The bony hand made a swing with the knife. Sam grabbed the arm in a vice-like grip, reared back, and pulled.

50

Many-Horses went to the table and wrapped his bleeding forearm with cloth and watched. Suddenly and loudly he said: "Woman! Sam. Woman!"

She was old and shriveled, with dark eyes that blazed with the ferocity and desperation of a wild animal. She tried to scratch Sam's face. She writhed, twisted, and kicked.

Sam wrenched the old woman to her feet and slammed her against the wall. He picked up the knife she had dropped, grabbed her by the shoulder, and slammed her to the ground. She spit and swore and snarled.

Sam leaned on the table. Many-Horses went over to block the doorless opening. He spoke in Spanish. The old crone cursed and shook both fists at him. He tried Navajo. She tried to spit on him.

Sam spoke in English. "Who are you? Where'd you come from?"

The old woman tried to spring up and attack Sam. He locked both arms around her, pinning her, took her outside, and slammed her into one of the chairs with oozing resin. He leaned with an erect finger inches from her face. "You settle down. You come within an ace of gettin' yourself shot. You settle down, or I'll break your neck."

The woman raised a filthy, tattered sleeve to wipe her mouth. She did not take her wild stare off his face. Many-Horses said: "She's goin' to spit."

Sam did not back away, and the old crone did not expectorate. Many-Horses studied the inside of their house when he said: "She was stealin' food."

Sam sat on the bench, facing the old woman. He shook his head. *How the hell does a man talk to someone who don't understand the talk?* He handed back the old woman's knife, haft first. She took it, and within moments it disappeared among her rags.

Sam said: "She's worse starved than you were, Many-Horses. Nothin' but skin'n bones."

Many-Horses raised the cloth. He was still bleeding. He spoke gutturally to the woman. She glared. Many-Horses went to take care of his injury. She watched every step he took. When he was gone, she looked defiantly at Sam and said: "Apache! Killer-people!"

Sam leaned with both hands between his knees. "He ain't Apache. He's Navajo."

"No good," she growled, and Sam almost smiled. "Your Injun?"

"No, ma'am. We're partners." Sam held the old woman's glare. "If you was hungry, all you had to do was come an' ask."

"No. No good white man, no good Apache!"

Sam eased back on the bench. "You Crow?"

She bristled. "Hidatsa!"

"You're a long way from home."

"Crow prisoner. Crow steal women. I kill two Crows to run away."

"How far is Crow camp?"

"Many days," she said, and raised an arm to point northward. "They move. Soldiers after them for reservation."

"What's your name?"

She said it first in Lakota then in English. "White Magpie."

Sam was briefly quiet. There was no such thing as a white magpie. When Many-Horses appeared, coming up from the creek, Sam said: "Her name is Bird."

The Navajo's response was tart. "With claws. Old bird with claws."

She twisted to watch Many-Horses where he stood, and, although the distance between them was considerable, she spat.

Many-Horses stood beside Sam's bench, looking steadily at the dark, ragged old woman before he said: "Where's your friend?"

White Magpie stared at Many-Horses without speaking. He addressed Sam. "She ain't by herself."

"How do you know?"

"Ask her."

Before Sam could speak, the old woman began another blistering attack in her own language. Neither of her listeners heeded the outburst. When she ran out of breath, Sam said: "Where is he? Hid back up yonder?"

Many-Horses said: "Chain her. I can back-track."

White Magpie sprang from the chair, letting loose another fiercely denunciatory barrage neither of her listeners understood.

Sam also arose. "Tell me where he's hid, or we find him without you."

She would have bolted, but in anticipation Sam grabbed the filthy rags and spun her to face him. They exchanged glares in silence. Many-Horses went into the cabin, returned with a rope, fashioned a slip knot, put the rope around the old woman's neck, and handed Sam, who had two good hands, the coil. Their chain was at the log landing. Sam explained that she would walk ahead, and, if she thought she could run, he would set back and strangle her.

She was reluctant. They had to prod her from behind several times. For a change she was silent. On the frontier the term was *sulling* — elsewhere it was called sulking.

She stopped where the forest began and looked back. Sam flicked the rope. Many-Horses did something else. He walked up beside the old woman. He saw that Sam had given her back the knife.

When they reached the landing, Many-Horses raised a hand. Where they halted, he quartered until he found the tracks. He went back to tell Sam they should chain the old woman. She turned on Many-Horses, but, before she could explode, he stepped up and with his uninjured hand slapped her face. She jumped back. Many-Horses shook his head. "No noise. No yell. Next time I cut your throat. *No yell!*"

They chained her on the ground with her back to a log they had abandoned because of its punky interior. She watched the Navajo go up where he had found sign. She ignored Sam. Many-Horses left the landing in a northerly direction. The old woman's lips were a bloodless slit, but she did not make a sound.

Once, when Many-Horses stopped, Sam quartered for sign and found none. When he returned, Many-Horses raised his unbandaged arm. "North."

Sam didn't ask, and the Navajo did not say how he knew. They paced soundlessly, Many-Horses out front. Both were armed with belt guns and long guns. Sam got close enough to whisper. "Bushwhack."

Many-Horses seemed not to have heard, but after another few hundred yards where the shadowy gloom was thickest he stopped. Sam stepped to one side, rifle in both hands. The silence was deafening. There was no movement. There were several huge old deadfalls. Many-Horses leaned aside his carbine, drew his belt gun, and changed course as he moved to avoid a huge old deadfall that had bear scrapings of bark and punk wood.

Sam remained to one side until they were beyond the dead forest giant, then exchanged a nod with the Indian, and they both turned to approach the deadfall from the north side. They stopped, waited for almost half an hour before they heard it, something in the abandoned bear den, making rustling sounds.

Sam put his rifle aside, leaned as far as he could across the deadfall. He found he could not lean far enough and gestured for Many-Horses to hold his ankles. It was difficult to get as far as Sam had to lean without making sounds, but he was as careful as he could be.

When he was far enough, so that all he had to do to look inside the log, he eased down with both hands, drew his six-gun, and leaned an inch at a time. There was an excellent prospect that the Indian in the den had heard them, had listened to Sam's coming down the far side.

Sam eased down the last six or eight inches with Many-Horses gripping his ankles, positioned his gun hand for instant use, and got the surprise of his life. The bear den's inhabitant was leaning in a straining position, looking outward and upward. Sam's gun barrel was a scant half foot away, the finger inside the trigger guard tightening.

They stared at each other for seconds before the den's inhabitant swung to knock Sam's gun aside and at the same time leaped forward to leave the den in a wild run. Sam instinctively grabbed and held on. He fell off the log and rolled for a better grip. His adversary fought like a cougar.

Many-Horses came around and moved without haste to pin the Indian by the arms. Sam let go, sat up, eased down the dog of his six-gun, and leaned against the deadfall, staring. Many-Horses had no difficulty pinning their captive, who strained and kicked, and jackknifed.

The Navajo looked over at Sam. "I don't think she steal food for buck, unless he was hurt. Bucks hunt, don't want woman help." Many-Horses yanked the fiercely struggling captive to its feet and held it at arm's length.

Sam arose dusted off, leathered his belt gun, and said: "It's a gawd damned child." He used a stiff finger to get the captive's attention. "How old are you?"

The captive tried to kick Many-Horses, swung one skinny arm, and, when Many-Horses caught it, he pushed the captive against the deadfall as he said: "You don't get hurt. We got your old woman."

56

Sam retrieved his rifle and leaned on it "It's a gawd damned female child," he said and squinted at Many-Horses. "What in the hell are you goin' to do . . . ?"

"Put belt around her neck," the Navajo interrupted to say.

Retracing their trail was no problem, but leading the prisoner was. She was harder to lead than a half-grown puppy.

CHAPTER
FIVE

Becerra

When the old woman saw them, she strained and howled in that language neither Sam nor Many-Horses understood. The skinny, dirty, and ragged child tried to rush to the old woman but was restrained. Many-Horses sat on a log. Sam yanked the captive back and pushed her to the ground. She and White Magpie kept up their gibberish.

Sam looked at Many-Horses. The Indian was thoughtfully considering the pair of captives. Eventually, as Sam arose to continue on their way, Many-Horses said: "Good circle," and ignored Sam's quizzical, scowling look as he hiked along behind the old woman and the child.

Sam saw the buffalo first. She was keeping a distance between herself and the hobbled horse. The horse ignored the buffalo. Andrew Cameron had heard them coming and was standing at the southwest corner of the cabin. When they came closer, he looked steadily at the pair of ragged, filthy Indians, spat, went back to the bench, and sat down.

Sam let Many-Horses follow the two female Indians inside the cabin. Cameron waited until Sam was seated, then disapprovingly wagged his head. Sam explained. Cameron got his pipe fired up, and, when the other white man was finished, the old cowman said: "The Army'll come for 'em. I'll get word to 'em. Injuns can't come here. Even my riders don't know about you'n this place."

Sam's reply was given after some thought. "If you take 'em to Boulder, there'll be an interpreter an' they'll tell about bein' caught up here, about me'n Many-Horses."

Andrew Cameron had to relight his pipe. When he had a good head of smoke rising, he removed the pipe and said: "Son of a bitch! All right, I won't send for the Army, but what're you goin' to do with 'em?"

Sam did not know. "We just caught 'em. They're wilder'n a pair of catamounts. That old witch cut Many-Horses and tried to cut me. I don't know. Maybe feed 'em up and run 'em off."

Cameron made a rueful, cold smile. "Like you done the buck? You feed 'em an' you'll never get rid of 'em. If you run 'em off, they'll hide out'n come back and raid you." Cameron brightened. "Do they speak English?"

"The old woman does, but she don't seem to like to do it. I don't know about the girl."

"Find out where they come from an' take 'em back."

Sam related what the old woman had told him — a Sioux caught by Crows and held prisoner until she used her knife to escape. He added a supposition. "She never said nothin' about the girl, but they was together."

Cameron considered his cold pipe and leaned to knock it clear of dottle. As he straightened back, he spoke dryly: "Crows are good sign trackers." He pocketed the little pipe. "They'll track 'em here."

Sam looked out to where the old buffalo was maintaining a distance from the big sorrel horse. "Like we talked some time back, I come lookin' for a special place. That's all."

Cameron leaned to arise. "You found a tree to make roof covering with?"

Sam shook his head. "We was searchin' when we come onto that old witch. Her name's White Magpie."

Cameron slowly nodded. "I saw one once, years back. All white feathers. Big as a chicken." He arose, turned to consider the roof rafters, went to the doorless opening, and stood with his back to Sam, watching the old woman and the child stuffing their mouths, using both hands from cooking pans Many-Horses had filled with cold stew. The Navajo looked up, but neither of the females did.

Cameron shook his head, went over to his saddlebags, dug in one pocket, and brought forth what looked like two round balls of tanned leather. He went back to the doorway and tossed them to Many-Horses.

The Navajo held them, nodded, and left the house bound for the creek. The old cowman told Sam that Navajos made only one kind of moccasins. When they were dry, they rolled them into balls, and, when they were needed, the People took them to water, soaked them soft, and put them on. They dried to size and fit.

60

"All your buck has to do now is take the buttons off his worn-out ones and fasten 'em to the new ones. After a day or so they'll dry to fit his feet." Cameron looked at Sam. "Damned pity we never learnt to do that."

Cameron went back to his mount, brought a croaker sack and left it inside the doorless opening against a wall, then returned to his horse, rigged him out in silence, and got astride, looking at Sam. "You wanted a private place to finish out your string of years . . ." He chuckled to himself and rode back the way he had come.

Many-Horses told the old woman by gestures for them to take the pans to the creek and clean them, then stood in the doorway, watching, as he told Sam that maybe White Magpie and the scrawny child would keep on going, maybe take the pots and pans with them.

Sam wagged his head. "What's in the sack?"

"Tinned food. Sam, why does that old man come up here?"

Sam Sloan had no answer.

White Magpie and the girl came back through tall grass. The old woman handed the cleansed cooking utensils to Many-Horses without looking at him, then went around the east side of the house. The little girl followed, but not until she had made a hint of a smile in Sam's direction.

Sam had wanted to find a sugar pine tree. It annoyed him that the old woman and the child had caused an interruption. He told Many-Horses he would go search, and Many-Horses could stay and watch the old woman and her companion.

Many-Horses did not dissent, but, as Sam walked northward, he watched, and, when the old woman came up to ask, Many-Horses told her in an inflectionless voice Sam was going to find a sugar pine tree so they could cover their roof.

White Magpie watched Sam walking as she said: "Wrong way. Sugar pine that way." She pointed easterly with a bony arm.

Many-Horses slowly turned. He wanted to say he did not believe the old crone knew a sugar pine from an alder. Instead he said: "How far?"

She made the *wibluta* sign for a walking person and held up two fingers.

When Many-Horses went back to the house, the old woman, now joined by the girl, followed him. They asked about the buffalo cow, so Many-Horses told them. White Magpie listened with obvious interest, went to the doorless opening, and looked out where the cow was curled up, resting under a hot sun. Over her shoulder she said: "White bird come to me in the night. I took Yellow Bluebell, and we ran three nights, hide three days. Keep to the night, hide in the suntime." She faced around. "Apaches have dreams?"

Many-Horses answered irritably. "I'm not *Apachu*. Nav-*ah*-ho! *Dineh*!"

"White man don't get dreams."

Many-Horses might have agreed. He was annoyed enough. Instead he said in Spanish: "*Yo no sé*" — I don't know — and shouldered past the old woman to stand in sunlight.

The girl said something to which the old woman answered curtly. She did not care whether she had angered the Apache or not.

Sam did not return until dusk. He entered the cabin, leaned his rifle aside, took Many-Horses by the arm, and led him to the creek where the buffalo cow was dripping water after drinking. She watched them without interest.

Sam fished in a pocket, brought forth mud, and knelt to wash it in the creek. He held up what remained. "Gold," he said.

Many-Horses picked up the largest yellow rock, hefted it, and put it back on Sam's palm. "Old woman say sugar pine trees long walk."

Sam let the hand lie in his lap as he looked steadily at the Indian. "Gold, Many-Horses. Up the creek at the rocky place we rested day before yesterday. I picked up the nearest pieces. There's more. I went in the creek half a mile where both sides are rocky." Sam paused to consider the expressionless face of the Indian. "You know what gold is, for Christ's sake?"

Many-Horses nodded. "Yellow dirt. *Dineh* make things. They hammer it."

Sam leaned back on his heels. "You old bastard, gold is better'n cartwheels. A man can get anythin' he wants with gold. There's more of it up yonder."

Many-Horses caught none of Sloan's enthusiasm. "We got to find sugar pine tree. Make old woman show us." He stood up. The old cow grazed close. He thought flies were around her. She needed more grease.

Sam pocketed the nuggets, walked back toward the cabin, alternately looking sidelong at the Indian and the grass, which was beginning to brown near the earth.

Many-Horses was never talkative. Now he was less so. Sam queried White Magpie about the sugar pines. She offered to show him.

The following morning early they struck out, each with food and weapons. The old woman was like a cricket. She was sinew and bone, did not seem to tire, but occasionally stopped to favor Yellow Bluebell. It was a long walk, much of it uphill, rocky in places and heavily timbered. When they began to slant downslope, the old woman told Sam: "Close now."

They hiked for another hour before reaching a sheltered place. Sugar pines grew among firs. There was also a scattering of pines.

The old woman led them to a fire-scorched ring of stones. It was the last camp she and the girl had made when they shared food. Beyond that place, as they angled northward, they found a few berry bushes and some wild onions, nothing else.

Sam and Many-Horses selected trees to fell. Sam thought Mr. Cameron might balk at dragging logs that far, but they felled three anyway, limbed, and left them. On the hike back, with night coming, Many-Horses followed their earlier sign even though dusk in the forest was turning to darkness.

They could not snake the trees to the meadow until Mr. Cameron returned, and, because Sam had no idea when that would be, he left the following morning before sunrise to go back up the creek.

Many-Horses did not respond when the old woman asked questions, so she avoided him, emptied the croaker sack, placed tinned food on shelves, and went twice to the doorway to look out where Many-Horses was greasing the buffalo. He did not return to eat. She told Yellow Bluebell the old Apache was sick.

Sam did not return. Many-Horses sat outside on the bench for a long time. Inside, the old woman and the child talked in bursts. The girl was afraid Crows would find them, and that made the old woman go out to tell Many-Horses Crows might have found Sam. Many-Horses said nothing when he got his old carbine, buckled his shell belt and pistol in place, and left the cabin.

White Magpie stood in shadows, watching Many-Horses heading for the path made from dragging trees. She told the girl Apaches could see in the dark.

Many-Horses used fading daylight to reach the creek and parallel it on the east side. As darkness settled, he increased his wariness. He was not convinced Crows would make more than a noisy, short search for the old woman and the girl, neither of whom would be worth much.

He paused several times, seeking scent of a fire, detected none, strained to catch sounds, but because of the creek he was not successful in that, either. He made slow, cautious progress and reached a rocky place where the creek's noisy tumbling over bedrock from higher up was too loud for other sounds to be discernible.

From what Sam had said, Many-Horses thought he had to be in the area where Sam had found gold. He moved with infinite slowness as far as the higher rocks where the noise was loudest, and stopped. Visibility was no more than fifteen or twenty feet. The noisy little waterfall overrode any other sound. Many-Horses climbed around the wet rocks, using the steel butt plate of his cavalry gun to prevent falling. When he was past the wet place, the creek widened, almost formed a roiling pool. Many-Horses found a mossy deadfall and sat on it. There was less noise here, but forest darkness cut visibility down to a yard or two. It occurred to him that further searching was pointless.

He was satisfied about the Crows. If they had come this far in their hunt, something he considered unlikely, Sam might have detected them and gone into hiding. He sighed, retrieved the old carbine from where he had leaned it, and stopped breathing. Something cold, hard and round was pressing into the back of his neck. Many-Horses did not move a muscle.

Sam holstered his pistol, came around to sit on the same rock, as he said: "Old bastard, how'd you get this far in the dark?"

Many-Horses gravely eyed the old buffalo hunter. "By smell," he said. "Now we go back."

Sam stood up. He was soaked to the knees. "That old witch will've taken everything she could pack and be gone."

Many-Horses arose, said nothing, and started back, using the creek as his guide. They reached the log landing where light from the heavens brightened the trail before Sam spoke again. "Tomorrow I'll take you up there."

Many-Horses walked almost to the clearing before replying. "You go. I care for old cow, work on house."

When they emerged in the vicinity of the cabin, a shrill, defiant voice stopped them. Neither understood what had been said, but Sam's supposition was wrong. The old woman had not run off. Sam said: "Talk English, you danged old heathen."

Her answer was in the same defiant tone. "Many-Horses lookin' for you."

The Navajo spoke softly. "I found him. He found me."

He led the way forward where the old woman was standing in the doorless opening, knife in one hand, club in the other hand. She barely yielded enough room for them to pass inside. Sam went to a candle and lighted it. Yellow Bluebell crawled from beneath a bunk.

Sam ignored her. He was hungry. There was cold stew and mealy potatoes. He ate both, and, sitting opposite him, Many-Horses emptied the pot.

Sam put the candle in the middle of the table and emptied his pockets. The old woman came close, made wet noises with her nearly toothless mouth, and spoke again in that alien language.

Many-Horses eyed the yellow rocks as Sam said: "Next time Mister Cameron comes up, I'll have a list for him an' give him gold to cover buyin' things."

White Magpie felt several of the stones, called them something in her own language, pulled the girl close, and made her look. Yellow Bluebell listened to the old woman, looked at Sam, and smiled. Many-Horses said he was tired, shed his shell belt and holstered pistol, went to his bunk, and bedded down.

Sam tucked the nuggets into a doeskin pouch which he took to bed with him. The old woman and Yellow Bluebell slept under blankets on the floor.

When dawn came, Many-Horses went out to grease the buffalo. He was out there so long Sam shouted to him from the cabin that it was time to eat. The old Navajo did not return for another hour by which time the sun was climbing. Sam had washed his nuggets at the creek and had lined them up on the table. He was smoking his pipe when Many-Horses returned. White Magpie handed him a tin plate of food. Many-Horses took it outside to the bench to eat. Sam followed him.

"You sick?" he asked.

"No."

"Somethin's eatin' you?" Sam sat on the arm of one of the chairs they had made of green wood. "You homesick? You want to leave?"

"No," the old Indian said, wiping up the remnants of meat juice from the tin plate. "We never named buffalo."

Sam frowned. "That's botherin' you? All right, name her."

"And calf," Many-Horses said, as he handed the plate to White Magpie.

Both the old woman and Sam stared. Slowly Sam looked out across the meadow. The old cow was lying in sun-heat.

Many-Horses said: "It's behind her. Little. Dog-size. I never seen one so little." He, too, looked out there. "Call her Old Mother."

White Magpie butted in. "Call her last *tatanka*." At Sam's blank look, she said: "Last buffalo."

Many-Horses nodded. "Her calf?"

White Magpie was holding the girl's hand in her withered claw. "What kind, bull or cow?"

"Cow calf," Many-Horses replied.

"Bluebell."

Sam said: "Maybe just Old Mother's calf." The three Indians, even the girl, looked disapprovingly at Sam. He told the old woman: "An easy name to say."

She nodded toward Many-Horses who gazed across the wide grassy place. "*Becerra*." At their blank looks he said: "Little girl calf."

Yellow Bluebell laughed. Neither Sam nor Many-Horses had seen her smile, let alone laugh. Sam smiled back. "Your *becerra*," he said and continued to smile. "Your *becerra*."

The old woman translated. The girl ran across the meadow.

Many-Horses softly smiled. He asked Sam what should be done with the animals. Sam gave a ready reply: "Let 'em stay."

Many-Horses looked upwards, then back down. "Much snow come."

Sam considered the Indian. "Old bastard, you always figure the worst."

Many-Horses arose and walked toward the distant buffalo, her calf, and the girl.

The old woman glared. "You treat him bad." She turned and entered the house.

Sam watched the old cow get to her feet and lower her head. Many-Horses called to the girl not to go close to the calf. He might as well have been talking to himself, but the old cow did not paw or make that rumbling bawl with her mouth open.

It was too late to make the trip up the creek, so Sam did other things. There was never a shortage of chores.

He ate when the old woman called to him. She, who seemed never at a loss for things to say, would not talk to him. Later, when he was piling kindling on the east side of the cabin where it was shady, she came out, watched briefly, then moved in to help. For a woman who had to be very old, she was strong, quick, and seemingly tireless.

He spoke to her several times. She did not answer until he said he thought Many-Horses was ailing. She stopped stacking to say: "Apache not sick. Apache unhappy."

Sam said: "He ain't Apache. He's Navajo."

She acted deaf. "He don't feel good."

"That's sick, ain't it?"

"No! He don't feel good you found yellow dirt." Sam straightened up and leaned backwards to ease his spine. The old woman spoke again. "He know yellow dirt bad."

70

Sam considered the old woman in silence before walking around to go inside where they had a dipper in a bucket of water. The old woman continued to rack up fat wood. Sam could hear her talking angrily to herself in her own language. He went out front to sit on the bench.

Many-Horses, Yellow Bluebell, and the cow buffalo were together out there. Sam had a twinge of something he hadn't felt since childhood — homesickness — not for a home he hadn't known, but for a family.

He went inside, rummaged for the whiskey, held up the bottle, and scowled. It was empty. The old woman appeared in the doorway, grinning from ear to ear. She said: "All go away."

CHAPTER
SIX

A Stranger, A Bird,
A Mouse

The old cowman returned astride his big sorrel horse. As usual he halted barely clear of the last trees. Sam saw him first. The old woman came out of the trees where she had been root hunting and stopped dead in her tracks. Yellow Bluebell cringed at the old woman's side.

Many-Horses was out with the buffalo cow. He looked back only when he heard Sam call a greeting. Andrew Cameron dropped a croaker sack, dismounted, off-saddled, led his horse out to be hobbled, and met the Navajo. They exchanged a nod and walked back together in silence.

The old woman and her companion came to the cabin. The girl ducked inside, but White Magpie gave stare for stare as Cameron offered tobacco so he and Sam could fire up. When White Magpie entered the cabin, the cowman said: "She's puttin' on weight."

Sam had not noticed, but he nodded.

Cameron pointed to the croaker sack. "Woman things. They look like a pair of scrawny scarecrows."

Many-Horses thanked the cowman for his moc-casins, which Cameron studied. The silver buttons were on each moccasin. Cameron said: "You got a white man name?"

Many-Horses replied quietly. "Old bastard."

Cameron's pipe emitted a puff of smoke as he looked at Sam. "You told me his name was Many-Horses."

Sam reddened. "It is."

Cameron did not pursue the topic. He told the Indian to take the sack inside and give it to the old woman. After Many-Horses was gone, Cameron said: "That's what you been callin' him?"

Sam was looking at the doorless opening where the Navajo had disappeared. Cameron had to relight his pipe before he said: "He knows what it means. Good buck, is he?"

Sam understood what the old cowman meant. "Just a way of talkin', Mister Cameron. You don't like Injuns."

"No! An' I got a reason." He changed the subject. "When are you goin' to cover them rafters?"

Sam explained about the sugar pines. The old man knocked his pipe empty and pocketed it. "Far, is it?"

"A long day's walk over, and the same comin' back."

Cameron arose, kinked his knees, and went out to bring in his horse. As he was saddling, he said: "Be back come sunup with an extra horse."

They watched him pass into the forest gloom and fade from sight. Sam turned as White Magpie appeared in the doorway, giggling self-consciously. The dress had no belt. It hung on her like a flour sack, but she was clearly pleased. She pushed Yellow Bluebell forward. Her dress lacked inches of touching the ground. It had two red ribbons, one just below each shoulder. She looked steadily at Sam. He smiled: "Down right pretty."

Yellow Bluebell went around the east side of the house and sat on the kindling pile. White Magpie asked why the man with big red horse didn't stay to eat.

Sam made no reply. Instead, he told Many-Horses he would shorten the girl's name to Belle. Many-Horses nodded. The old woman didn't like it, but Sam and Many-Horses called her Belle anyway.

Andrew Cameron returned the following day before sunrise. It would take all day to snake the sugar pine logs to the easterly slope of the timber above the meadow. He had brought his big sorrel and an even larger Roman-nosed brown horse with little pig eyes that had trouble getting the logs started, but, once they moved, he did not stop even for a breather until Sam unchained him above the meadow. Eventually there was only one log left.

While they were resting, before returning for that one, Cameron told Sam and Many-Horses the pig-eyed big animal took pulling as a personal challenge. "Danged simpleton'd try to pull a mountain until his shoulders'd give out. I brought rolled barley for 'im. Let's fetch that last log."

Many-Horses remained behind when Sam and the cowman went after the last log. On the way Cameron said: "I brought a splittin' wedge an' a hand maul. You'll have enough shakes for the roof an' leftovers. You ever split shakes?"

74

"No."

"Many-Horses has."

Sam did not question that statement.

The sun was setting by the time they unchained the last log. Dusk had turned to dark by the time Many-Horses was ready to take the horses out to graze.

Cameron said: "Wait."

He got a small sack from a saddlebag, fed both horses the rolled barley, then nodded for Many-Horses to take them away.

White Magpie appeared in the doorway. "Eat," she announced.

The girl in her new dress with the pair of red ribbons brought the last pan from the outside cooking hole. As she passed the cowman, she made a shy smile and surprised both white men when she said: "Thank you," pronouncing each word carefully.

White Magpie had two candles lighted. Normally only one was used. They had three left of the six the cowman had brought earlier.

Cameron, as a cowman, was a meat-eater. The old woman had spiced the meat with plants from the forest, herbs, and roots. He looked up once. "Good," he said and went back to eating.

When the men went outside, Cameron asked Many-Horses to bring in his horses, and, after the Indian departed, Cameron said: "You got two too many."

Sam was stuffing his pipe. By the time he had it fired up, he had forgotten what the cowman had said, went inside, and returned with a heavy small pouch which he handed to the cowman.

Cameron hefted the sack, went inside, and loosened the pucker string beside a candle. For a long time he rolled nuggets between his fingers before putting them back in the sack. He looked up at Sam who had followed him inside. "I don't need it."

Sloan's answer was brief. "Pay for what you done for me. Next time, I'll have more."

Cameron went outside, rigged out his sorrel, and made a squaw bridle with which to lead the pig-eyed brown horse. He leaned without mounting for a long moment before looking around at Sam.

"You got a good source?" he asked.

"Good . . . as far as I know."

"Mister Sloan, this here is raw gold."

"Buy Many-Horses a decent Winchester, an', if there's anythin' left, a Colt hand gun."

Cameron almost imperceptibly nodded. "Anythin' else?"

"Maybe some geegaws for the women."

"You?"

"I got all I need," Sam said. "More'n I figured on. If there's anythin' left, it goes toward what I owe you."

Cameron got astride, picked up the slack to his lead-animal, and headed for the timber.

Many-Horses was up where they had left the sugar pine logs. As the cowman rode past, Many-Horses made a tentative salute, and to his surprise Andrew Cameron returned the gesture.

Sam and the old Navajo went up to draw-knife the logs and worked by moonlight until late. When the last log was stripped of bark, Many-Horses sat on it, ignored the sticky sap, and gazed out over the meadow at the cabin, at a thin tendril of smoke rising from the west side of the house where White Magpie had her cooking hole.

Sam sat beside him. "Start splittin' tomorrow?"

"Better split when wood dry, but we can't wait. Grass is turnin' brown at roots." Many-Horses arose. "Get plenty wet splittin' new wood."

They returned to the cabin, and White Magpie met them, sniffed, and pointed to the pair of resin-sap chairs. "You sit."

They sat.

The old woman and the girl brought food from the inside table. Many-Horses smiled. "She don't want us to set at table with pitch on pants."

Sam learned what the old Navajo meant the following day after they had cut the logs to the length Many-Horses marked with a hand axe. The took turns splitting shakes. Many-Horses showed Sam how to make fairly uniform wedges. By midday they were both soaked from splitting green wood. It was hot, but where they worked there was tree shade. Once, when they stopped for water, Sam asked how Many-Horses knew about splitting shakes.

"Learn at mission. They hired me out to soldiers for roofing long-houses."

They finished with one tree by late afternoon and went out to the creek to wash. Resin was impervious to water, but they washed anyway. When the girl came with a bucket, she went upstream and would not look at either of them, not even when she arose to go back with the water. The only time she relaxed was when she was with the old woman, who watched over her like a hawk.

It required four days to finish making shakes and to carry armloads down to the cabin. White Magpie watched them, and, when they brought about half of what they had made, she shook her head. "Too wet. No good." She went to the north side of the cabin and returned with fat wood kindling. "This dry wood. Burn hot. Not wet."

Many-Horses took several shakes, placed them together on the ground, and pointed to the rafters. The old woman looked up and shrugged as she went around to her cooking hole.

When they had the shakes piled, the old woman told them to give her their clothes. Many-Horses complied, but Sam did not. He went around to the cooking hole, watched the old woman swirl Many-Horses' britches and shirt in boiling water, remove them with her stick, and place them flat out on the ground. She spoke curtly to the girl, who used a flat stick to work the resin off.

Sam gave the old woman only his shirt. He would not part with his britches. White Magpie covered her nearly toothless mouth and laughed. Sam was inside the cabin when Many-Horses appeared in the doorway to say there was a rider up the southeasterly slope on the trail Andrew Cameron used. He said it was not Cameron.

Sam went as far as the door to look up there but saw nothing. Many-Horses was gone. So was his old Sharps carbine.

Sam called for his shirt. When White Magpie brought it, it had been scraped but was still wet. He put it on and had difficulty making the bone buttons stay in their button holes.

It was a hot day. There were thunderheads moving west at a snail's pace. They occasionally covered the sun. Sam waited for one of those interludes and loped toward the easterly rise which was covered with timber.

He did not find Many-Horses, but he found something else: shod horse tracks where a rider had paralleled the meadow while remaining hidden by trees. He coursed for the rider without finding him. Afternoon sunlight shone brightly down across the park, but only an occasional streak of it penetrated to the forest floor as Sam tracked. He paused where the sign veered westerly, and Many-Horses came from behind a huge fir tree. He gestured that the rider was angling toward the creek. The same thought hit them both at the same time. The stranger was looking for the waterfall where Sam had found gold.

Sam asked if Many-Horses was sure it hadn't been Cameron. The old Indian was sure.

They tracked until they could hear water, then parted, and, while keeping each other in sight, used forest gloom, rough barked old trees, every shadow to hide their approach. Their stealth provided no result. The horseman was not in sight.

They went to the creek, found where he had watered his animal and scouted, and had afterwards splashed on across. They tracked him until it became clear he was traveling southward to parallel the west side of the meadow. They followed the tracks, did not see the rider, and, when they reached the park, rested briefly before starting across toward the house. The buffalo cow bunted her calf to the rear and stood defensively as the men hiked past.

The sun was sinking. Long shadows reached part way across the park. White Magpie fed them outside. Sam's britches stuck to everything he sat on.

She brought an unopened bottle Andrew Cameron had left inside the croaker sack. It was swaddled like a baby. Sam opened it, swallowed twice, and pushed it toward the Navajo who regarded the bottle dourly and shook his head. White Magpie swooped up the bottle and returned it to its hiding place in the cabin.

Sam was loading his pipe when Many-Horses said: "Now trouble." He looked Sam in the eye. "Yellow dirt bring trouble."

Sam smoked in long silence, until Yellow Bluebell returned from the creek with a bucket of water, then he said: "Did you see him?"

Many-Horses's reply was curt. "Only his back. Once. Big man on bay horse."

Sam let the pipe go out. "How'd he know about us in this place? How did he know to ride up the creek?"

Many-Horses did not reply. Eventually he went out to the old cow with his empty peach can half full of grease. Sam remained on the bench as dusk darkened to night, then went inside where the old woman had one candle lighted. She looked up quickly, then looked away. Yellow Bluebell did not look at Sam.

Many-Horses returned, shelved his can, exchanged a sharp glance with the old woman, and sat opposite Sam at the table. "He will come back. We could go up there, hide'n wait."

Sam sat back, eyeing Many-Horses. Association made people close regardless of differences. He smiled at the old Indian. Before heading for his bunk, he said: "I'm glad you come."

They left early the following morning, found an excellent hiding place, and waited. The horseman did not appear. With evening coming, they returned to the house where White Magpie fed them in stony silence.

The following morning they worked at sheathing the rafters, alternately watching the side hill and laying sheathing. Neither of them had much to say. For Sam Sloan the possibility of someone discovering his gold strike impaired his efficiency on the roof. The source of Many-Horses's brooding silence had little to do with gold. When they had to stop work because of failing daylight, the old bronco took his tin of grease and went out where the cow was suckling her runty calf. He sat in tall grass, ignoring the shaggy old animal and her baby. Only once did he look at her. That was when he said: "Circle broken," and washed both hands in the creek. When the cow was dry and the calf circled for a bedding place, he went over and greased her wounds, which were healing well. She was filling out, but she would never be able to store fat under her hide as she had once been able to do.

She stood perfectly still as though she understood what the old Indian was doing. Helping her. And, for a fact, blowflies hadn't been able to lay their eggs in the wounds.

By the time Many-Horses returned, the candle had been snuffed out, and the people inside bedded down. As he noiselessly sidled around the young girl, White Magpie's claw-like hand gripped his ankle.

He stopped, looking down. The old woman whispered something he could not understand. He knelt beside her blankets. She came partly upwards and spoke in English, but in so low a tone, if the night hadn't been deathly still, he would not have been able to hear.

She said: "Bird come."

Many-Horses leaned closer. "Spirit bird?"

"Yes."

"Dream vision?"

"Yes."

"Do I want to know what it told you?"

This time the answer was not only delayed, it was spoken in an almost inaudible whisper. "It say to me in strange language. It say blood comes with the full moon."

Many-Horses gazed steadily into the shriveled face of the old woman before getting to his feet and going to his bunk.

The following morning they did not work on the roof until afternoon. They spent the morning coursing, first south then north, for a rider. Even the tracks were filling in. There were no new ones.

They returned to spend what remained of the day on the roof. White Magpie climbed their notched post to help. Sam sent her back down to her cooking hole. Many-Horses finished only when it became too dark to see.

At supper with one candle on the table Sam said: "Maybe it was a grub-line rider, maybe a feller lost in the timber."

Many-Horses gazed across the table in silence before resuming his meal.

Sam said: "Yeah," and also went back to eating.

Yellow Bluebell came timidly to Sam's side and held out her hand. A small, wet mouse was on her palm.

White Magpie said: "Found it in the creek. She needs something."

Sam smiled at the child. "Keep it dry. There's some grain in that sack Mister Cameron used to feed his horses. Put it in there."

The girl's face glowed. She said: "Thank you," so expertly Many-Horses knew the old woman had coached her.

Sam returned to his meal, paused when he saw the old woman watching him, and said: "Is she Crow?"

"No, Crow slave. She been afraid all day you would kill the mouse."

Sam's eyebrows shot up a notch. "A mouse?"

"White man kill."

Sam gazed at the Navajo, who did not raise his eyes. He was busy finishing supper.

They went outside, all but the child. She was busy making a nest in the little grain sack for her mouse. Many-Horses gazed at a scimitar moon. White Magpie watched him doing this. Neither of their faces showed anything. Sam wondered aloud about the mysterious horseman.

The Indians remained silent. Eventually, when it was time to bed down, Sam went inside to his bunk. The girl was sound asleep with the little feed sack beside her.

Now in his bunk Many-Horses arose, looking upwards.

The old woman softly said: "Many days."

He answered without lowering his gaze. "Your bird should have talked of gold."

"Why?"

He finally faced her. "It brings poison."

"Maybe bird come tonight. I ask it about gold."

Many-Horses gazed at the old woman, went back over to his bunk, and spoke in darkness. "*Dineh* make webs to trap night visitors. Spider web traps."

White Magpie's reply was tinged with doubt. "Vision bird will fly through any trap."

Many-Horses bedded down but lay awake, looking up past the sheathing to talk to the stars. Not exactly to the stars which were only small holes that let a higher light show through. He talked to the stars because his words would go through them.

CHAPTER
SEVEN

Days Of Summer

They did not search for the rider for many days. It was slow, tedious work, boring through shakes for slivers of bone to hold them to the sheathing. Only once did Sam leave with his rifle to return to the little waterfall and its area of moist stones. Many-Horses told the old woman white men were worriers, and she agreed without knowing, or particularly caring, if this was so.

When Sam returned, it was dark. He had used that scimitar moon as a guide. They had eaten. The child was feeding her mouse whose wildness had vanished. It ran up and down her arm, nuzzled her face, and hunkered on her hand when she fed it.

Many-Horses did not ask what Sam had found, if anything. He looked upwards and jutted his jaw. It was now possible to see the sky in only one place, near the ridgepole. Sam finished eating. "Finish tomorrow," he told the Navajo. "You did a sight of work today."

Many-Horses glanced in the old woman's direction. "Good helper."

They went outside. Sam sat in one of the chairs. Many-Horses sat on the bench, still covered with tree

85

limbs. Many-Horses would have sat in silence all night. What was said would have to originate with Sam. When he had a good head of smoke rising from his pipe, he said: "No sign of him." He fished in a pocket, leaned to hold a palm where Many-Horses could see it. "I never knew it was that easy. Where the water runs, there's gold. I'd guess, bein' heavy, it sinks."

Many-Horses eyed the nuggets, several as large as a pigeon's egg. When he leaned back, he gazed out where the buffalo was without saying a word.

Sam pocketed the gold and also looked out yonder. "Is she healin' well?"

Many-Horses nodded. "Calf's too little. Old cow don't make much milk." The Navajo returned his attention to Sam, gazing solemnly until the girl brought her mouse to show Sam how tame it was. After she went back inside, Sam cocked his head a little. "Is a mouse a bad omen to your people? You sure been quiet lately."

The old Indian looked up where that scimitar moon was appearing and disappearing among broken clouds. "Mouse lives in ground where Spider Woman came out. My fingers are stiff from making bone nails," he said, and arose to go inside.

White Magpie was waiting. The light of one candle smoothed out enough wrinkles so that she looked much younger. She spoke quietly to Many-Horses. "Bird don't come back."

He was tired enough to head for his bunk, as he replied: "Maybe tonight."

The ensuing two days Sam and Many-Horses worked on the roof. Only a sliver was left to do when White Magpie called them down to eat.

The girl sat at the table with the mouse on her shoulder. She fed it greens and pine nuts, which it shelled while near her ear. She called it a name neither Sam nor Many-Horses understood and could not pronounce.

Later, when Sam went out to the bench to smoke, the old woman came out. She perched on the arm of one of the sticky chairs. She clearly wanted to talk, so Sam made it easy for her. He said: "Girls have dolls. Is that mouse her doll?"

White Magpie almost smiled. "The mouse is baby to her."

Sam shifted position and examined the bowl of his pipe. He did not like the way this conversation was going, but, when he looked up, he said: "She's no more'n a baby herself."

White Magpie was a long time in speaking again. "You have wife, children?"

Sam let the pipe go out. "No."

"I have three girls . . . never seen them after Crow raid. Big now . . . somewhere . . . got men now . . . maybe babies of their own."

Sam crossed and uncrossed his legs. "Someday, maybe . . ."

"No! Dream bird tell me no." White Magpie looked steadily at Sam. "This one my child."

Sam nodded while relighting his pipe. He was not expecting what the old woman said next.

"She no child now. She woman."

Sam frowned. "What'n hell are you talkin' about? She's no more'n eight or ten years old. She won't be a woman for . . ."

"Years no matter. Girl becomes woman when it is time."

Sam neither fully understood nor wanted to, so he knocked the pipe empty, pocketed it, and stood up. "We got to finish the roof tomorrow."

The old woman did not move. "You dumb," she said, arose, and passed Sam. She entered the cabin, and, by the time he entered, she was deeply under blankets on the floor next to the girl.

It was drizzling when Sam and Many-Horses arose. Water only entered the length of the ridge pole. Otherwise it was dry inside. Sam spoke from the doorway. "One more damned day," he exclaimed.

Many-Horses went farther out to look at where the buffalo and her calf ignored the rainfall. The rain suited him, not entirely because it would renew the meadow grass, but also because his back ached, his hands were swollen, and the mouse with the unpronounceable Crow name had spent most of the night under his blankets, exploring.

White Magpie cooked at her hole in the ground, as though rain was unavoidable. She motioned to Sam to send the girl to her. He turned and said: "Belle?"

The girl did not immediately respond. She still wasn't used to her shortened name. Sam gestured. "White Magpie wants you."

The girl tucked the mouse inside her clothing and went outside. Sam shook his head. When the cowman returned, he would give him gold to fetch back a doll.

It rained steadily for two days, a soft, warm, summer shower. White Magpie eventually used a blanket when she worked at the cooking hole. Sam was restless, but Many-Horses joined the old woman at the fire hole, also wrapped in a blanket, first face forward, hands outstretched, then with his back to the fire.

He and the old woman talked with long intervals of quiet between sentences. She knew his name but did not use it. She persisted in calling him an Apache. Many-Horses had flared up about that once. Now, when she said it, he simply would not look at her or answer her questions.

The morning of the third day sunlight came, the ground steamed, and the creek overflowed. Many-Horses eyed Sam with sidelong glances.

When Sam took his rifle and left the meadow, Many-Horses climbed to the roof and laid shakes. His hands worked well enough until the heat up there became uncomfortable. He had finished, except for a small area near the back wall, climbed down, and shouldered the old woman away from the cooking fire to extend his arms and flex swollen fingers.

White Magpie watched in silence. When she could leave the cooking to Belle, she disappeared up the east slope and was soaked to the knees when she returned. This time it was White Magpie who shouldered the Navajo from the fire. Whatever she was cooking made Many-Horses and Belle wrinkle their noses.

It was a hot day and did not cool off by late afternoon. White Magpie took the girl up the creek almost to the drag-trail where they bathed. She sat on a rock to dry, watching the girl playing in the water. Their peace was interrupted by a gunshot. The old woman yanked the girl by the hair. They fled toward the nearest cover, which was the first tier of big trees. White Magpie handed the girl her dress and told her to put it on.

Many-Horses also heard the gunshot and with his old carbine ran up the westerly hill to have high ground from which to watch. There was no second gunshot, nor was there movement or sound. Many-Horses began coursing northward. Eventually he altered course in the direction of the skid-trail. White Magpie saw him and signaled with an upraised arm. He did not go to her. He continued upcountry like a wraith, moving only when he had examined every yard of the gloomy, dripping forest.

When he saw Sam, the old buffalo hunter was carrying something over his shoulder. Many-Horses got closer and whistled. Sam stopped, dropped his burden, and waited. When Many-Horses materialized, Sam was wiping blood off his shirt. The old bronco looked from Sam's load to Sam without speaking.

Sam continued skiving blood off as he said: "Bear."

Many-Horses nodded about something that was obvious. No animal had hair that coarse and color except a bear. He said: "Where's the rest of him?"

Sam bent down to wipe blood off his hands on the ground. "Back up yonder, beside the creek." Sam

90

straightened up to dry his hands down the side of his britches. "The feller who shot him must've passed the house in the dark."

Many-Horses went closer to examine the haunch. Sam wagged his head. "That chunk of meat weighs as much as me."

"Did you see him?"

"All I seen after the gunshot was a horse runnin' like the devil was after him. I never seen his rider. My guess is that the bear rose up out of the rocks, or come from behind a tree, and scairt the livin' daylights out of the horse, an' he run out from under the feller who shot the bear. Lend a hand hoistin' that meat."

"You cut it off the bear?"

Sam threw an annoyed look at Many-Horses. "They was gone, the man an' his horse. Him likely tryin' to catch the horse. They was gone, plumb gone, so I cut off a haunch. Help me hoist it."

Many-Horses strained. They got the dead weight back into place, with Sam straining, and started in the direction of the cabin. White Magpie and the girl came out of hiding to join them. Not a question was asked, not a word was said, until Sam dropped the meat near the cooking hole. He then explained to the old woman how he had come by the haunch and told the girl to use the old woman's fleshing knife and remove the hide, with an admonition not to allow hair to taint the meat by touching it.

The old woman led the way into the cabin, unwrapped the bottle, and handed it to Sam, as she said: "Wash shirt again . . . gawd damn."

The women cooked meat all afternoon, late into the night, and the following morning. Even with dehydrated meat — jerky — there was no assurance the meat would not spoil, especially during the season of warmth.

Sam went shirtless for the second time. When he and Many-Horses were considering that open place on the roof, Sam told the old Indian what conclusion he had come to about the persistent stranger.

"Kill him. Hunt him down no matter how many days it takes, an' kill him."

That had been Many-Horses idea the first time, but that time, too, they had not found the stranger.

The following morning Sam's shirt was not quite dry and smelled of the smoke arising from the cooking meat. Belle came to the doorway while the men were eating, followed by White Magpie. What the girl said the men did not understand, but White Magpie's rigidly raised arm was understandable even before she said: "Horse!"

The saddle was under the horse's belly and both reins had been broken off from being stepped on. The horse was cropping grass around its bit. Neither the horse nor the buffalo paid much attention to each other, which meant the horse had arrived on the meadow earlier, during the night.

Many-Horses would have gone out to them, but Sam stopped him. "He's out there, most likely in the yonder trees. He's found his horse. He's got to come into the open to get him."

White Magpie returned to her cooking hole. The girl went with her. There was still meat to be dried. Neither of them paid any attention to the yonder horse or the fringe of westerly forest. Sam wanted to remove the bridle so the horse could graze better, but he didn't, and, when the sun was nearing its meridian, the horse drank at the creek, and then stood hip-shot, dozing, with the buffalo cow keeping a distance.

Many-Horses said: "He come in the dark."

Sam smiled. "So will we."

The women came around from the cooking hole, sweating like stud horses and carrying smoked meat that looked like old shriveled leather. Belle hunted for her mouse. It was up among the rafters with some pine nuts which it shelled with disregard of those below.

White Magpie said: "Flies don't go in dark," and knelt down to pile the dehydrated bear meat under Sam's bunk. Both the men were interested in the lowering sun. Both had belt knives as well as holstered pistols. White Magpie added: "Apache good horse thief. They come in night. Sioux, Crow, no go out in night."

Many-Horses sounded irritated when he said: "This one no Injun. White man." At the old woman's skeptical look Many-Horses said: "White man saddle!"

The old woman did not speak again. By now both men had learned that, once she made a statement, she did not pursue it.

Sam watched the sun. So did Many-Horses but his gaze was more somber. When the moon came, it would be slightly fuller.

White Magpie pushed past to return to her cooking hole. She busied herself, banking coals and rearranging firewood. When she returned, she told the men there was a man slightly south of the cabin in the yonder forest. "He smokes."

Sam and Many-Horses exchanged a look. The old woman had to have a nose like a bear to detect tobacco scent at that distance.

They ate with the sun showing pink from dust in the air as it settled lower. This time of year it would not sink completely until later. Belle stood in the doorway, stiffened, and turned to speak to the old woman, who went swiftly to the door. The horse was gone! She barked at the men who came to the doorway.

Sam said: "Son of a bitch!" to which the old woman replied: "Apache! Crawl through tall grass. Apache good horse thief." She smiled at Many-Horses, pushed past to go back to the table, and watch. Belle was playing with the mouse.

Sam was angry enough to arm himself and strike out in plain sight across the meadow. Many-Horses waited, old cavalry carbine resting over a forearm at the corner of the cabin, but there was no movement, no stealthy shadow, no sighting of a rider. Eventually Many-Horses also crossed the meadow. Sam pointed to crawl marks, the same marks when the caught horse had been led back among the trees.

They had no difficulty reading the sign, but it was getting along. Dusk would arrive shortly, and, where Sam halted, Many-Horses nodded without speaking.

They would not find the stranger. From this point on he had loped the horse.

When they appeared as soundless phantoms in front of the doorway, the old woman spoke from behind them. She had a club. "He no come back." She followed them inside, lighted a candle, leaned her club aside, and peered at them. "Crow, maybe," she said.

Sam shook his head. "White man."

"Scout? Hunter?"

Sam and Many-Horses exchanged a look before Sam said: "Maybe," and arose to head for his bunk. As he passed the girl, the mouse on her loose hair watched him.

Before blowing the candle out, the old woman fixed Many-Horses with a bright stare. "Bird no come."

"Maybe tonight," he muttered, arising.

"Bird come no more. Bird no like Apache."

Many-Horses was tired. His hands were bothering him again. He stood a moment, looking stonily at the old woman, then went to his bunk.

For the following three days they scouted for fresh sign. There was none. Their next project put them in a position where they could watch the westerly timbered slope while they made a door out of split logs. For hinges they used double folds of stiffening bear hide.

The fourth day the mouse was missing. Belle searched every crack and dark place. The old woman crooned to her, combed her hair, and spoke softly in Crow. Many-Horses told the old woman to explain about the pain that came throughout life, told her to say the mouse had to go her own path. Be happy, the mouse had brought sunlight into her life — because only rarely did anything like that happen.

The fifth day Sam left in the dark. The others did not know he was gone until dawn. The old woman said: "Hunt. Scout."

Many-Horses did not comment. He worked outside where they piled fat wood and watched northward. He had no difficulty understanding where Sam had gone. Yellow dirt got inside the brain. Even some Indians became infected, but mostly it was whites.

With the sun directly overhead the old Navajo went with his peach can out where the old cow was standing, head hung, soaking up warmth. The calf was curled into a ball in front of her.

She scented him before hearing him, raised her head, both black eyes wide, knew who he was, and let her head sag. There were bug-hunting larks in the grass which fled at sight of Many-Horses. He watched the largest bird, muttered, and approached the cow to apply grease.

Her cougar scars were healing well but slowly. Fast healing was for the young. The old healed slowly. He talked to the cow who did not even look at him. He rubbed grease into his hands and flexed them. He told her summer would fade. Winter would come, and she did not have enough teeth to find graze through snow. He told her he had done what he could, had wanted her last summer to be good.

He sat down beside the calf. For a few moments the cow watched him, then relaxed and closed her eyes again. He told the sleeping calf it would have to die when snow came. It was runty. Snow piled up. It was slick, sassy, and in good flesh, but it would not live beyond this warm time.

He sat a long while, listening to the creek and batting at deer flies. He had many years to go back through, many lives, many hurts, and a few pleasures. At his feet something rustled grass.

Very cautiously he parted the grass with one hand, moving slowly and carefully. The tiny mouse raised her head when a passing hand bared her nest. He lowered a sore hand slowly. She hopped onto and off of it. She became partially hidden in grass. Many-Horses heard the tiny squeaks, leaned closer, slid a hand beneath the nest, and lifted it. The mouse clung to her nest. Many-Horses arose and started toward the house, one hand cupped over the other hand.

When he stood in the doorway, White Magpie looked from his face to his hands. He went closer and lifted the cupped hand. White Magpie made an almost indistinguishable trilling sound and went to the door where she called until the girl appeared. Many-Horses was sitting at the table, the nest in one half-closed hand. When Belle came close, he told her to put her hand down, and sure enough the mother mouse ran up her arm to her shoulder and back down.

White Magpie asked: "How many?"

Belle's voice lilted when she replied in Crow. The old woman rolled her eyes. "Four and the mother."

Many-Horses arose as he addressed the old woman. "Big grassy place, very little mouse. Maybe she was waiting for me . . . or for her."

He went outside where he had heard someone walking. Sam leaned aside the rifle. He was dripping sweat, but, before going inside to the bucket and dipper, he held out a filthy hand with broken fingernails.

This time *each* of the six nuggets on his palm was as large as a pigeon's egg.

CHAPTER
EIGHT

The Scrawny Man

They heard him coming, but, because he had never before arrived except in early morning, Many-Horses and Sam left the cabin and positioned themselves with guns. The old woman who could detect tobacco smoke over a considerable distance evidently could maybe see in the dark. He was midway down the east slope when she hissed at Sam. "Old white man on red horse."

Cameron neither nodded nor spoke as he dismounted and let Many-Horses care for his animal. He had two heavy croaker sacks. Sam helped by carrying one sack inside where White Magpie lighted a second candle.

The grizzled old cowman looked steadily at Sam while removing his roping gloves and folding them over his shell belt. He jutted his jaw toward the sacks. "That's what you wanted an' maybe a little more. Where's the girl?"

She was motionless in a corner where light did not reach. White Magpie addressed her in Crow. She came forward timidly, clearly frightened. The mouse was on her shoulder, whiskers nervously twitching.

Andrew Cameron sat at the table and held out a work-roughened hand. He neither smiled nor spoke.

White Magpie leaned to look, then straightened as she spoke in Crow again, and Belle took two reluctant steps and stopped when there was enough light by which to see.

Her eyes widened. She darted a look at the forbidding face of the old cowman, another look at White Magpie who spoke sharply to her in Crow. Belle did not move, so the old woman took the gold necklace from Cameron's hand and put it over the girl's head, then stepped back, and spoke softly.

Belle's dark gaze did not leave the cowman's face as she meticulously said: "Thank . . . you."

Cameron arose and with his back to the others began emptying the sacks. He handed Sam the new Winchester and the Colt revolver, still blue from the factory. With his back to the others he emptied both sacks, then jerked his head for Sam to follow him outside.

It was a warm night, and a slightly fuller moon made visibility adequate at close range. Cameron filled and lighted his pipe, saw Many-Horses returning from the meadow, and said: "You trust him?"

Sam nodded. "With my life."

The cowman waited until Many-Horses came up and dropped the bridle. Cameron pointed to a chair. Many-Horses perched on the arm.

Cameron removed the pipe and looked into its bowl as he began speaking. "I figured it would happen. In Boulder there ain't an assay office. It's been gone a long time. I got your supplies at the general store. Paid with your nuggets. I've known that storekeeper since he came into the country thirty years back. I seen the look on his face when I give him the rocks to be weighed. I told him I'd found 'em at an old worn-out sluice nine miles southeast of Boulder. I told him I'd take it kindly if he wouldn't say a word." Cameron paused to refire the pipe. "He said he wouldn't. If I hadn't known him so long, an' if I hadn't known his words was good, I'd never have used the gold for the supplies."

Sam was holding an empty pipe in one hand and made no move to fill it. "Mister Cameron, there's been a rider nosin' around the last few weeks. We never got a good look at him, but a bear spooked his horse. He shot the bear, but the horse loped. One mornin' it was out yonder, grazin'."

"What was its brand?" Cameron asked, leaning forward slightly as he asked the question.

"We never got that close, an' somehow he crept out there an' got the horse."

"You tracked him?"

"Southerly until it got too dark."

The grizzled cowman refired his pipe. Eventually he said: "Well now, that's interestin'. I thought it was Alex Manning at the store." He arose. "I ain't ate since mornin'."

Inside the cabin White Magpie had slices of dehydrated, smoked bear meat with which she fed the men. Belle was back in her dark corner, showing the necklace to the mouse. Many-Horses and the old woman exchanged a long glance before White Magpie went to refill tin cups with coffee as black as Original Sin.

Andrew Cameron eventually pushed the tin plate aside and leaned on the table, scowling slightly at Sam. "Been my experience, Mister Sloan, that folks can damned nigh smell gold. If you got one snooper, sure as I'm settin' here, you'll have others." Cameron pulled back from the table and made a death's head smile. "You should've walked in some other direction, or maybe farther into the mountains."

Sam had no comment to make, so he fished out six nuggets and placed them in front of the old cowman, who flicked a look at Many-Horses and White Magpie before fondling the gold as he dryly spoke. "You're about as old as I am, so you'd ought to know folks learn about gold strikes."

Sam flared up. "She's never left here, an' neither has Many-Horses. I'll bet you a handful of gold it's the storekeeper. He'd have nuggets to show folks."

Cameron emptied his cup, made a grudging nod at the old woman, and arose. "I need them sacks," he said and faced Many-Horses. "I'd take it kindly if you'd fetch my horse."

In poor light the Navajo had not seen the new guns, not even as he passed them on his way out. Cameron gazed after him — and wagged his head. Old convictions died hard. Sometimes they never died.

He and Sam went back outside where Cameron sat on the bench through a long silence before he said: "I'm beginnin' to suspicion somethin', Mister Sloan." If he had intended to say more, something happened that shocked both old men into stunned silence. Yellow

Bluebell came out, marched like a soldier to the bench, leaned, and pecked Cameron on an unshaven cheek.

He sat frozen for five seconds. When he turned, the girl had fled back. From the doorway White Magpie made a wicked smile, patted the girl's head, and told her in Crow that was how whites expected children, even young women, to show gratitude.

Belle went back to her dark corner where light did not show the high color in her cheeks. She got very busy feeding pine nuts to the mouse that, White Magpie had told her, needed the nuts to make milk for her babies.

When Many-Horses brought in the big sorrel horse, Andrew Cameron got his bridle, bitted the horse, pitched his saddle blanket over its back, and flung up the saddle. As he reached under for the cinch, he spoke gruffly to Many-Horses. "Inside in the front corner . . . new guns," and snugged up the cinch with Many-Horses watching from an expressionless face.

As soon as the old cowman was astride, heading up the slope, Many-Horses ducked inside. Sam was in the doorway when he began a long harangue in Navajo-Mex as he examined the weapons in better light.

White Magpie said: "No talk Apache."

Many-Horses turned, broadly smiling. "Damn' fool woman . . . *¡Navajo! ¡No Apachu!*"

She let go a loud sigh and began cleaning up after the meal.

Many-Horses, who usually slept like the dead, did not do so this night. He had the Winchester and the Colt on the bunk with him.

Sam helped the old woman sort out and shelve the supplies. When he came across four cartons of bullets, two for the hand gun and two for the Winchester, he went over to place them with the guns on the bunk. Belle came out of her dark place to show Sam her necklace. It was beautiful. In the center was a *naja*.

The following day Many-Horses, the only one who could, explained what a *naja* was. When he and Sam were outside, the Navajo cradling his Winchester in one arm like a baby, he gave further details about *najas* which Sam had never heard before, and, while he listened, he was not greatly interested.

They made winter wood for ten days. It was hard but necessary work. By Sam's estimate they would require between three and four cords to see them through the cold time.

That night Many-Horses went to the creek to soak his hands in mud, and the calf nuzzled him. He paid no attention to the calf. He watched the cow. Buffaloes had unpredictable temperaments. In some circumstances they would do something cattle rarely did. They would fight a man on a horse. They had trampled their share of men on foot. But the old cow simply watched.

Sam disappeared three days in a row and returned with a leather parfleche the old woman had made for him, a dead weight with its load. Many-Horses was beginning to believe the stranger on the bay horse would not reappear. He had something else on his mind and suggested to Sam that they make a three-sided shed for the old cow and her calf.

Surprisingly, Sam agreed. They felled small trees, limbed, skinned them, and used improvised shoulder harnesses of rope to drag them to the place Many-Horses thought they should make their shed.

White Magpie helped. One evening, when Sam and Many-Horses were washing at the creek, Sam asked the question which had become Many-Horses's main anxiety. Sam said: "We got no scythes to cut hay for 'em. No sense in fixin' a place for 'em, if there ain't nothin' to keep 'em alive come three-foot snow drifts."

Many-Horses asked if Sam knew how to use a scythe. Sam did. He'd hired on to put up winter feed for stockmen several times in his life. As he arose, drying both hands on his shirt, he said: "Next time Mister Cameron comes up, we'll trade him gold for scythes."

Two days later Many-Horses took his peach tin out to apply grease and told the old cow she might not have to starve to death, after all. She stood patiently motionless while Many-Horses slathered her, watching her calf play as though the Navajo was not there.

They shaked the shed roof and still had shakes left over. White Magpie did not like having the shed close to her cooking hole. She complained that it would block breezes from the north. Both men agreed with her and went hunting.

Belle's mouse could not control her offspring, once they started exploring. Many-Horses and Sam could be upcountry, making wood, and still hear the old woman when she found a baby mouse in one of her cooking pans.

Several times, as days passed, Sam noticed Many-Horses going outside after supper to gaze steadily for long periods at the moon. Once he went out and also looked up, as he said: "Autumn's a long way off," and returned to the cabin, leaving Many-Horses out there. Several nights the old woman came and stood in silence, also looking up. When Many-Horses met her gaze, she would return to the cabin without speaking.

It rained again — for three days this time. The shed roof leaked. After the weather improved, they climbed up there with slivered shakes, found the leaks, and pushed the widths of thin sugar pine where the leaks had been. The roof would not leak again — for a very long time anyway.

The mysterious rider reappeared, this time skirting the meadow from the far side, but the buffalo cow and her calf stood like statues, and Many-Horses told Sam someone was over yonder. When the horseman passed a place where slivers of sunlight shone past the tree tops, they saw him, only briefly, before he blended with the forest gloom.

They got their guns from the cabin and, under the anxious gaze of the women, reached the timber on the east side and trotted. The rider would be ahead of them, which was better than their being ahead of him. It was breathlessly hot even in the forest. When Sam stopped to listen, then resumed the hunt, they went slowly and cautiously.

Sam saw him first, where he dismounted on the west side of the creek and led his animal by one rein, as he slowly paced beside the waterway. Sam whispered, "Lookin'," which the stranger was indeed doing.

He stopped often to scuff at the water's edge with his boot. Once he knelt and, using both hands, got wet almost to the elbows, sifting the shallows. Sam had seen enough. He was about to move when Many-Horses touched his shoulder to whisper, "Not him. Different one."

Sam went soundlessly ahead and gestured for Many-Horses to move off to one side. The horse either saw movement or picked up scent. The man was sifting wet mud and did not see the horse peering across the creek, little ears forward.

Sam halted in the last fringe of trees. Many-Horses was several yards southward when he stepped on a wet stone and slipped. The stranger's head came up. Both his hands were frozen with wet mud, sifting through the fingers. He very slowly stood up, very slowly wiped both hands down the outside of his britches. The horse shifted stance. The man looked back for a brief time, then faced forward again. He slowly yanked loose the tie-down over his holstered Colt.

Sam did the same. He also drew his sidearm. The only sound was made by the creek. The stranger was not as thick and burly as the other stranger, and he was clean-shaven. He was a wiry, shockle-headed individual. Sam cocked his hand gun. Whether or not the stranger could hear that sound across the creek was doubtful, but he rested his right hand on the saw-handle grip of his sidearm.

Sam spoke. "Shuck the pistol."

The stranger's head turned a fraction in the direction of the voice. He appeared unable to see Sam where the timber was thick and solidly shadowed.

Sam repeated it, slightly louder this time. "Drop the gun!"

The lean, sinewy man obeyed. His pistol fell in mud. He peered intently in the direction of Sam's voice, as Sam told Many-Horses to keep watch and moved into the stranger's sight to ford the creek, cocked hand gun aimed low and as steady as stone.

Sam was half a head taller than the stranger. When they were close, Sam said: "What you doin' up here?"

The stranger was not a good liar. His eyes shifted when he said: "Lookin' for cattle an' got lost."

Sam glanced at the horse. "Huntin' cattle with a carbine?"

"Well, there's likely bears and cougar up here."

"What's your name?"

"John Smith. What's yours?"

Sam spun the man half around and pushed hard. John Smith sprawled in the creek, sat up, sputtered, and began clawing toward the east side where Many-Horses appeared, holding his new Winchester low in both hands. The stranger stopped. Many-Horses made a point of letting him see it when the Indian cocked his carbine.

Sam waded out and grabbed the stranger's shoulder, grunted hard, and hurled him into the mud on the east side bank. The stranger did not arise except to get into a sitting position. He rubbed water from his eyes, considered the new Winchester staring him in the face, and briefly coughed, then swore.

108

Sam said: "Stay there," recrossed the creek, got the horse, and midway back across yanked the stranger's carbine from its saddle boot and dropped it in the water. Not another word was said as Sam pulled the stranger to his feet and punched him hard over the kidneys to start him walking.

Sam could have ridden. Instead he led the horse, which was a leaned-down using animal in top shape and not too old. When they reached the clearing, White Magpie and Belle stood in cabin shadows, watching. The girl clutched her necklace in both hands. The old woman made a bitter, keening high laugh. When the men were close enough, she berated the soaked stranger in a language none of the men understood but did not have to. What the old woman did was denounce the soaked stranger, calling him names in two languages, Lakota and Crow.

They took him around front where Sam pushed him into one of the chairs, leaned his rifle aside, and said: "You, John Smith son of a bitch, you lie one more time an' I'll scalp you down to the bone. You understand!" When John Smith was slow to nod, Sam leaned and backhanded him across the face.

John Smith said: "I understand."

Many-Horses went inside to lean aside his Winchester, drink from the bucket, and return to the doorway, chewing a strip of bear jerky as tough as a boiled owl.

Sam pointed to the horse. "Where'd you get it!"

"Out'n the remuda where I work."

"Where do you work?"

"I ride for Andrew Cameron. That's his mark on the horse. Big connected A C on the left shoulder."

Sam sat on the bench. "What you doin' up here?"

Many-Horses drew his fleshing knife to cut off the strip of jerky protruding from his mouth. He held the knife still, awaiting the stranger's answer. The stranger looked from the old Navajo's expressionless face to the poised knife and replied to Sam.

"A feller said there was gold up in here. Past the cabin a mile, or such a matter, along the creek."

"What feller?"

"Billy Grover. He rides for Mister Cameron, too."

"Big, thick, hairy feller?" Sam asked, and John Smith nodded. "Why did he tell you that?"

"He knew, that's all he said. He knew there was gold up here, most likely along the creek. Lots of it."

"You his partner?"

"Yes. Me'n Billy partnered on a dozen cow outfits. We come back to the Cameron outfit three years, straight runnin'. The old man's hard to like, but he pays good and mostly leaves his riders to do work they know inside an' out." John Smith paused to watch Many-Horses sheath his knife. He was not a large man, and, soaking wet, he looked like a half-drowned rat. He began speaking again. "Billy said I'd know I was goin' right when I come to a park with an old buffalo cow with a calf in it. He said to keep clear of the house."

Sam leaned a little. "What is your name?" he asked, articulating each word carefully. It sounded like a threat, and evidently John Smith thought it was, because he answered promptly: "Jed Carville."

110

"Mister Carville, does Mister Cameron know you fellers ride up here when you're supposed to be huntin' sore-footed bulls an' hung-up heifers?"

"He don't boss much. We been with him before. We know the chores."

"But you ride up here."

"Well, he figures we're out doin' a day's work. Sometimes he rides along but not a whole lot." The Cameron rider leaned back in the chair. It was hot, and he was drying out fast. He considered Many-Horses, White Magpie, and Sam. He did not see Belle because she was in her dark corner with her pets.

He began speaking again, almost as though he were among friends. He told them about Billy Grover's returning in the wee hours, using his belt for a rein, straddling a saddle that had been mauled, things Billy had no difficulty hiding from the old man. He also told them all the Cameron riders were curious about the old man's going and coming, mostly with hidden things and once using a pack horse.

Sam said: "So they followed."

"No. Luc wouldn't. He said it wasn't none of our business."

"Luke a Cameron rider?"

"Yes."

Sam and Many-Horses took Jed Carville around the east side of the house and chained him there. He whined and groveled and protested. They went back around front to hobble the Cameron horse and turn it loose on the meadow.

CHAPTER NINE

The Shadow Of Trouble

Sam told the old Indian they had a problem. White Magpie spoke from the doorway in a matter-of-fact tone of voice. "Bury him."

Many-Horses twisted to gaze at a rising moon. It was not yet dusk; nevertheless it was up there. When he faced back around, he said: "Give him to old cowman."

Sam nodded. The problem was they never knew when the old cowman would appear, so they made a pallet outside, where he was chained. White Magpie fed him and gave him a Lakota name which only she understood. It was *dina sica*. It meant no good.

The buffalo calf gave its mother fits. It would run like the wind, tail over its back like a scorpion. It would charge directly at the cabin and at the last moment change course. Many-Horses laughed at it. He said they should call it *loco en cabeza* which in border Mex meant crazy in the head.

Sam went less often up to the little waterfall. He had the parfleche full of washed yellow dirt and had half filled that little sack Mister Cameron had left behind after feeding rolled barley to the horses.

One cool afternoon with cloud galleons moving from south to north at a snail's pace — which meant rain — Belle came from the creek, put the water bucket aside, and ran to White Magpie in tears. A large greenish grass snake had swallowed two of the baby mice.

When Sam and Many-Horses returned from hunting, carrying a pronghorn antelope between them, White Magpie told them why the girl was crying in her dark corner. Sam went to work, skinning the pronghorn. Many-Horses went inside to sit with the girl. It was problematical how much of his border English she understood, but there was no mistaking the sympathetic tone of his voice.

When he returned to the west side of the house, close to the cooking hole, and rolled up both sleeves to help with the skinning and gutting, he said nothing. Sam thought nothing about it. The last few weeks Many-Horses, who had never been talkative, had become less so. He spent more time out with the old cow and her calf. It butted, backed off, curled its tail high, put all its weight aft, and charged him. It was getting heavy enough to bowl the old Indian over.

Sam spent time on the cabin's east side with their chained captive. Since it was obvious he would be unable to escape, and the lanky old buffalo hunter occasionally brought him coffee, some chewing tobacco, and kept his water bottle full, they formed a kind of friendship. Jed Carville had ridden for outfits Sam had known. Once the prisoner told Sam his absence would be noticed, and he was right. Two days later the old cowman appeared on the easterly slope, sitting his big sorrel horse, ignoring the people below, concentrating his attention on the horse in the meadow.

When he eventually rode down, Carville hailed him. The old man ignored the rider, off-mounted in front of the cabin where Sam and Many-Horses were waiting, handed his reins to the Navajo, and looked straight at Sam. "What you got him chained for?"

Sam explained. Cameron went to the bench and sat down, watching Many-Horses hobbling the sorrel horse. When he eventually faced toward Sam, he said: "Well, I told you, folks can scent it up." He fished for his little pipe and went to work tamping shag into the bowl. "Billy Grover, eh?"

Sam sat in one of the chairs and waited. When the old man had the pipe fired up, he squinted through blue smoke and growled: "Billy. I wondered why he got back to the yard late." He stood up. Sam followed him around where Jed Carville looked up, showing a crooked smile.

Cameron puffed a moment before removing the pipe to speak. "How'd Billy figure to come up here? Don't lie, Jed."

"He followed you. Left off ridin' with the rest of us an' follered you. He told me you'd made a trail a blind man could foller."

"How'd he know about the gold?"

"Scraped around in your saddlebags an' found some dust flakes an' a nugget."

Andrew Cameron had a prominent vein in the side of his neck which swelled. "That'll account for the missin' nugget when I got to town . . . Luc, too?"

"No sir, Mister Cameron. Luc said it was none of our business if you rode off into the mountains."

The grizzled cowman stood smoking and staring at the man chained to the log wall. Without another word he jerked his head for Sam to follow and went back to the bench and chairs. Many-Horses was holding his new carbine. Before he could say anything, Cameron shot him a look and said: "I don't want to hear nothin' about it," and sank heavily down on the bench. Many-Horses took the Winchester back inside and leaned it. White Magpie said something he did not understand and grinned like a tame ape.

Later, Sam explained to Many-Horses that Mister Cameron got uncomfortable when folks thanked him. Many-Horses accepted that and never again mentioned gratitude for the guns.

Cameron ate with the others in silence, his tufted brows pinched together in thought. Not until Belle came from her dark place to tell him about the grass snake eating two of her mouse's babies did the old, stone-set face loosen. He asked White Magpie how much English the girl understood.

White Magpie surprised both Sam and Many-Horses when she replied: "She learn fast. I teach her every day. No let her talk Crow, make her put white man's words together." White Magpie looked at the girl. "Tell him how old you are."

Yellow Bluebell replied without hesitation. "Sixteen years."

Sam with a forkful of bear meat stew half way to his mouth stared, slowly drifted his gaze to the old woman who nodded just once and went outside, taking the girl with her.

Many-Horses broke the silence. "Little girl no more."

Cameron reached for the dented tin cup with coffee in it, looked over the rim at Sam, and spoke as he lowered the cup. "I figured her maybe eight or ten. Even in the dress with red ribbons she don't push out like a woman."

Sam had not noticed any change, but Sam like Andrew Cameron had taken it for granted, as skinny and scrawny as she had always been, that she was much younger than sixteen. He said: "Maybe her'n White Magpie didn't count right."

Many-Horses said: "Remember the time the old woman come back from the creek with her an' talked to you . . . an' called you dumb?"

Sam remembered but did not reply. He, like the cowman, went back to eating.

When the meal was finished, Cameron shoved tin plates aside and looked steadily at the sinewy old buffalo hunter. "I come up here to see what you figured to do with that old buffler cow. She can't make it through the winter. Her'n the calf."

Sam mentioned scythes and put gold nuggets in front of Cameron, who looked at them with a scowl.

116

When he spoke, he did not mention scythes. "Is she broke to lead?"

Many-Horses looked at the cowman. "Buffalo don't lead like horses."

Sam agreed. If he did not possess broad knowledge of many things, he knew a lot about bison. "I once knew a feller who raised one from a baby. It would lead good. He even got it to let him ride it. But that old girl out yonder won't drive, an' by my lights no one could teach her . . . not even Many-Horses, an' him'n that cow are closer'n a man an' a dog."

Cameron turned toward the Navajo. "Would she follow you?"

Many-Horses did not hesitate. "No." Then he asked why Cameron wanted to know these things, and the cowman answered in his usual gruff manner.

"You fellers can cut meadow hay with scythes until the cows come home an' not get enough. That old girl's calf is growin'. If we get a real Norther come winter . . ." Cameron did not finish; he simply shook his head at Sam. Then he explained about his questions. "If she could be drove down to lower country, she could run with my cattle. I've seen cattle an' buffaloes grazin' together. An old man told me they smell pretty much alike, so they get along."

Sam thought he and Many-Horses would have to palaver about this. Since the Indian had done more for the old cow, and she tolerated him, perhaps even liked him, they would have to talk. Sam changed the subject.

"You want that feller, chained to the house?"

For several long seconds Cameron gazed at Sam without answering, before he made a rough sigh and leaned back off the table. "Ponder on it," he said, and then answered Sam's question. "I don't want the son of a bitch. Nor Billy Grover. But I can tell you somethin' about Billy. He's got a tongue that's hinged in the middle and wags at both ends. I don't know about Jed, but him'n Billy partner together. If them two run loose, Mister Sloan, you're goin' to have more folks up here with sluice pans an' picks than you can count."

White Magpie appeared in the doorway. She and Belle both had armloads of kindling wood. They had been on their way around to the cabin's west side, where the cooking hole was, and had heard part of what the men at the table had said. She stopped, shifted both scrawny arms for a better grip on the fat wood, and said: "Bury him."

She disappeared around the side of the cabin as did Belle, who avoided looking at the men at the table.

Sam wagged his head slightly. "Only thing I can figure is to keep him chained up here."

Many-Horses asked: "How long?"

Both Sam and Cameron understood, but neither spoke for a long time. During the silence they could hear White Magpie around by the cooking hole enunciating words in English, not once but many times until they heard Yellow Bluebell repeat the words.

Cameron arose, ran thick bent fingers through his mat of gray hair, and said: "You got to ponder about the buffalo. I got to ponder about Carville."

He went outside where the sun was low enough to have a pinkish tint. Instead of sending Many-Horses out to fetch back his sorrel, Cameron went out there with the Indian. They stood a long time, gazing at the old cow, who gazed back for a while, then dropped her head to crop grass.

Cameron said: "She's old."

Many-Horses replied without hesitation. "Everything up here old, except girl, an' she will be old."

Cameron considered the wrinkled, gnarled old Indian and laughed. The first time he'd laughed in a long time. They led the sorrel horse back together. Many-Horses wanted to thank Cameron for the guns. He recalled Sam's admonition and only said: "Old cavalry gun never shoot straight and make smoke."

Cameron understood perfectly, said nothing the rest of the way back, then held out his forearm. Many-Horses grasped it briefly before walking away.

As Cameron was rigging out his horse, he spoke aside to Sam who was standing nearby. "I expect there's good ones." Without explaining what he meant, he turned the sorrel once, then swung into the saddle. He was evening the reins when he also said: "Let that son of a bitch starve for all I care," and nudged the horse into a walk, heading up the slope.

When dusk arrived, Sam and Many-Horses went outside to palaver. Many-Horses liked the cowman's offer to take the buffalo cow and her calf to lower grass country. That was not on Sam's mind. He said: "I expected he'd take Carville back with him."

Many-Horses put a guileless gaze upon Sam when he spoke. "He only have one horse." At the annoyed look he got from Sam, he added a little more. "He found no yellow dirt. Dug in creek, scuffed rocks. No gold."

Sam's frown dissolved. "He'd tell his partner there's no gold?"

"He find none. He dig in mud an' found none."

Sam fished for his pipe, stuffed it, lighted it, and spoke through a bluish, fragrant cloud. "His partner did . . . in the cowman's saddlebags."

Many-Horses was skeptical. "All whiskers found was a bear. Lost his horse."

Sam smoked in thought. If Many-Horses was right . . . ? But the burly man with whiskers had made several trips. He removed the pipe to say: "Whiskers knows. He got a nugget."

Many-Horses said nothing. As far as he was concerned, they had found no gold. He arose to go inside for two pulls from the whiskey bottle. It was something he disliked doing, not entirely because what it did to Indians he had seen lying unconscious, but because it did not taste good. However, it did have one beneficial effect — within fifteen minutes both his hands and his back would stop hurting.

Sam took the tin plate from White Magpie, went around on the cabin's east side, and hunkered as he handed the food to the man chained to the wall. Carville mumbled thanks and filled his mouth, chewed, and looked pensively at Sam. After swallowing, he said: "I heard what Mister Cameron said, an' I worked steady for him for three years."

120

Sam let that remark pass. "Somethin' I got to tell you, Jed. There ain't no gold up here."

Carville stopped chewing.

Sam allowed no interruption. "That dust an' rock your partner found in Mister Cameron's saddlebags come from the sluice of an old mine Mister Cameron found southeast of Boulder."

Carville resumed chewing, but slowly. He looked steadily at the sinewy old man. Eventually he swallowed. "Billy follered Mister Cameron up here an' scouted up the forest an' all. He said he found boot tracks along the creek."

Sam did not argue. He told Carville to go to Boulder and talk to the storekeeper. Then he arose and freed Carville's chains. "Your horse is out in the meadow."

Carville rubbed his wrists, went to the corner of the cabin where he could see the horse, then turned. "If you're lyin', Billy'll kill you."

"Take Billy to see the storekeeper. Go get the horse."

As the scrawny rangeman started in the direction of his horse, both Many-Horses and White Magpie came up and watched Carville briefly, before Many-Horses turned slowly and put a quizzical look at Sam.

Sloan watched Carville leading his horse back to be bridled and saddled. He did not say a word. White Magpie snarled under her breath in that language neither Sam nor Many-Horses understood and stiffly stood in the doorway, skinny arms folded over her chest as she watched the rangeman rig out, get astride, and nod stiffly to Sam.

By the time Carville was topping out up the easterly slope among the trees, Sam jerked his head. They went to the table where he sat, explaining what he had done. How and why he had done it.

White Magpie's disapproval was unrelenting. She said the rangemen would be back. She also said her idea was best — bury them.

Many-Horses, with very little pain in his back or hands, considered Sam in long silence before asking if Mister Cameron would like Sam's setting Carville free. Sam's answer was brief. "If he don't, when Carville goes back for his pay, Mister Cameron can bury him."

Belle came out of her dark place. Another of the baby mice had disappeared. Many-Horses told her mice grew up very fast and left their mother to become hunters. The girl went back to her corner, determined that the last little mouse would not leave. She fixed it a little bed which its mother chewed into fluff. Both mice bedded down in it.

The day after Carville's departure White Magpie went into the forest for edibles. Belle remained at the cabin. The old woman was like a ghost, soundless, constantly moving, probing and searching. She straightened up from a mushroom bed to face a large young Indian with roached hair. A Crow! His carbine was sheathed in a buckskin scabbard. He also had an old pistol, a knife, and a tamiaxe. He had two painted stripes on his face, across his nose and around the curve of each cheek. He eyed the old woman without expression.

122

She stopped breathing for several seconds. The buck was young, muscular, and confident. He asked her who lived in the house where the old buffalo was. She told him an Apache and an old white man lived there. She and a young girl also lived there. Then, now over her fright, she asked his name and why he was so far from Crow country.

He relaxed as he replied. Soldiers had found his village. There had been a fight. There were too many soldiers. When he had run out of bullets, he had fled, had been traveling west for six days. White Magpie asked if he had food. The buck nodded. He asked if she had seen soldiers. When she lied, she looked him straight in the eyes. There were companies of soldiers, she told him, Indian hunters, some on foot, some on horseback. She raised a thin arm. "Go south. There is open country. Watch for them. Down there go west."

He asked if she was Crow, and she lied again. She said she was not only Crow but the woman of Lone Bear, to which the buck replied that Lone Bear had been killed in a fight months ago. He smiled, nodded, and moved soundlessly southward.

When White Magpie got back, she told Many-Horses and Sam of the encounter. Sam wondered if there were more fleeing Crows. He said none of them should go far from the house, and the following early morning, when White Magpie came to grab Sam's sleeve, he went to the door with her.

It was the cowman on his big sorrel horse.

They told him of the old woman's meeting, and Cameron watched the Navajo taking his horse out to be hobbled in the meadow as he spoke in a dry, matter-of-fact voice. "I saw moccasin sign down lower. Maybe it was the old woman's Injun."

"Did you see him?" Sam asked.

The grizzled rancher put a bleak look on Sloan. "You don't see 'em unless they want you to. When I get back, I'll take the riders an' see if we can find him." Cameron got comfortable on the bench, while Sam explained about releasing Carville, how and why he had done it.

The old man spat amber, repositioned his cud, and asked Sam how many nuggets he had given him.

Sam answered shortly. "Six."

The cowman ruminated a moment before speaking. "I was sure it was six, but, when I got to the store in town, I only had five."

They might have pursued this if Many-Horses hadn't returned. He dropped the bridle beside Cameron's chair and said: "Shadow movin' across the meadow."

Sam arose, as did Andrew Cameron. Sam got his rifle. "Sure as hell it's White Magpie's Injun."

Cameron sifted through his saddlery, yanked out a carbine, and growled. "Horse-stealin' son of a bitch, an' my sorrel's out there in plain sight."

Many-Horses got his new Winchester. White Magpie asked what he was doing. Many-Horses did not reply. He stepped outside to join the other men. Cameron asked where Many-Horses had seen the wraith, and, when the Navajo replied, the cowman craned around toward the easterly slope beyond the cabin and jerked his head.

In the timber it was cool. Sam led, using a wide stride. Cameron, old as he was, grizzled and gnarled, kept pace beside Many-Horses.

If the cowman had no idea where Sam was leading them, Many-Horses did — in the usual roundabout way to the creek. When they could hear water, Sam stopped. Before he spoke, Many-Horses drifted southward. Sam told Cameron to scout in the other direction and not to make a sound. The old cowman sank down, removed his spurs, draped them from a low limb, and remained in tree gloom as he went on a zigzag course northward.

CHAPTER
TEN

The Escape

It bothered Many-Horses that, when they could see the creek through timber, there was neither a man nor a horse in sight. If the shadow he had seen had been seeking the creek, maybe the little waterfall, he'd had plenty of time to find them both. A mounted man, especially if he were moving, would be visible, despite forest gloom. He hunkered and waited until Sam appeared, then the old Indian told Sam what he thought.

They scouted for Cameron, found him sitting on the ground with his back to a deadfall, carbine across his lap, sound asleep! Sam leaned to make a low, barely audible whistle. Cameron's eyes snapped open. He started to raise the carbine as he turned. Sam said: "He's had plenty of time."

Cameron got to his feet, dusted off, and loudly said: "Son of a bitch!" — and without another word brushed past Sam and the Indian, taking long strides back the way they had come.

They reached the landing with its drying curls of draw-knifed shavings underfoot when the cowman moved easterly into timber and speckled shadows.

126

When they halted again with most of the southerly meadow in sight, Cameron watched the buffalo cow before speaking. "He's in the house. Be real careful." He led them closer to the easterly rim above the cabin and stopped again. "A man gets old, he forgets," he said, and jutted his jaw down in the direction of the house without an explanation.

Many-Horses eased his Winchester to the ground and leaned on it. Cameron addressed the Indian. "You know what he done?"

Many-Horses gravely inclined his head, gazing at the cabin where there was neither movement nor sound.

Sam spoke for the first time since they'd left the creek. "If he's in there . . . ?"

Before he could finish, the cowman growled: "You can bet your life on it, Mister Sloan. He ain't the best rangeman I ever hired, but he's *coyote*. He'll be rummagin' for your cache, an', if he don't find it directly, that girl'n the old witch will be screamin'."

Cameron looked at Many-Horses. "You're the tomahawk. Tell us how you snuck up on settlers in broad daylight."

Many-Horses said nothing for a long time, not until Sam started to speak, then he replied without looking away from the cabin. "I never snuck up on settlers. I snuck up on horses."

Sam remembered Cameron's saying they should put a window in the north wall, which they had not done. In fact, they had not cut windows in any of the walls. He said: "Gettin' down there won't be hard but gettin' inside will."

They descended warily, despite the impossibility of the rangeman in the house being able to see in a northerly direction. Where they stopped, beside the mound of dry grass made by White Magpie which she used in conjunction with fat wood to start cooking fires, Many-Horses pressed the side of his head against the logs. When Cameron would have whispered, the Indian raised a hand for silence. He could hear a man's voice, but the words were indistinguishable. He pressed harder. This time the high-pitched sound of a female voice, speaking English, was discernible. He listened until the man spoke, then pulled back to say: "Old woman mad. She say, if he touch girl, she kill him."

Sam stood briefly in thought before pointing to the mound of cured grass and, without speaking, groped among the fat wood until he found sticks the length he wanted. He took several to the mound of grass and went to work. Many-Horses and the cowman watched briefly, before joining Sam. The only comment was made by Many-Horses when he said it had worked at the bee tree.

They were diverted by the sound of a bunk being wrenched from the wall. They worked faster. When they had half a dozen torches ready, Cameron said: "The door opens to the right. Can it be barred from the inside?"

Sam shook his head. "It's got a wood lift. Just squeeze it."

Cameron nodded. "I'll go around get in front, an', when you show yourselves on the east corner, I'll yank it open."

After the cowman left, Many-Horses said: "Tough old man."

Sam said nothing. The voices inside were louder. The man sounded furious. The old woman's voice was not as loud but was clearly defiant.

Sam and Many-Horses crept to the southeast corner and peeked around. They saw the door but no sign of Andrew Cameron. When they pulled back, Many-Horses said: "Takes more time for him."

They waited. There was the sound of more destruction inside. Shelves were being torn from the wall. Tinned and bottled food hit the floor with force. The man was raging again as he upended the table and kicked the benches over.

Many-Horses peered around the logs. The cowman was in place. Many-Horses pulled back, re-gripped his three grass bundles wrapped to a piece of kindling, and, when Sam softly said — "He's ready" — Many-Horses got a lucifer from Sloan, lighted the first torch, the second, and third torches, handed them to Sam, and lighted two torches for himself.

The grass caught quickly. Sam leaned and nodded. Cameron soundlessly approached the door, gripped the *tranca*, and shot Sam a glance, before squeezing the handhold so that the bar inside would raise.

Cameron flung the door open and ducked back. The door struck the wall as Sam crept close, pitched in the first firebrand, then the second and third ones. He sprang back as Many-Horses came around, torches blazing. Many-Horses pitched in the first torch and leaned to do the same with the second when gunfire erupted inside. The old Indian dropped the second torch. Sam picked it up and hurled it inside, then turned. Many-Horses was sitting on the ground with his back to the east side front wall. Sam started toward him, when another burst of gunfire came from inside, where thick smoke made visibility and breathing difficult. This time the gunfire seemed to be upwards toward the roof.

Cameron yelled for the man to come out. The smoke was so thick anyone emerging from the cabin would be difficult to make out. Cameron had his back to the opposite front wall from where Sam was when he yelled.

Three more shots came from inside, slowly spaced — one — two — three.

The man inside could not see. He was making perfunctory, searching shots. Cameron yelled. "Come out before the smoke strangles you!"

He got no reply, and there were no more gunshots. Sam surmised the man inside must have found Many-Horses's cartons of bullets. He had been shooting randomly as fast as he could haul back the dog and snug up the trigger.

Smoke billowed past the open door. Cameron jumped ahead and slammed the door closed. Within minutes more random gunshots preceded the man inside violently kicking the door open.

Cameron called again. "Let the women come out first!"

Again there was no reply, so the cowman swore mightily and told the forted-up man they were going to

130

burn him out. Sam speculated their enemy would not believe it. All he had to do was look around. The entire cabin had been erected of green wood.

The torches were dying. Dry grass burned furiously and smokily but not for long. The smoke would linger, if it had only one outlet, the front door. That much smoke would not dissipate quickly.

Sam glanced back at Many-Horses. He got a solemn look in return. Sam motioned for Cameron to get as close as he could and empty his hand gun into the smoke.

After the cowman had done that, Sam sprang past the doorway, raised his hand gun, searching for the man who had caused all this. A squeaky voice from far back said: "He gone."

Sam found the old woman crouching in front of Yellow Bluebell, who was terrified. Both women had tears down their cheeks. Sam's eyes stung, too.

White Magpie pointed upwards, where smoke was escaping through a large hole, the place where he and Many-Horses had done the final finishing. Below the hole two sturdy rafters, roughly twenty-four inches apart, had provided perfect footing.

The old woman coughed into a rag over her mouth which she lowered enough to say: "Shoot hole an' climb out."

Sam yelled to Andrew Cameron, who hurried to the southeast corner of the house where the slope was visible. He got a fleeting glimpse of someone running up there and fired. Behind him Many-Horses said: "Sam go after him."

Cameron turned and looked down, saw the blood, and yelled for Sam to go up the slope. Cameron turned back, knelt, and pulled the old Indian's hands away from his front. There was blood, a large amount of it, and fresh.

Cameron swore, went inside, groping for a cloth. The old woman helped. She talked rapid fire as she helped in the search. When she found a clean cloth, she turned and barked in the direction of Yellow Bluebell's corner, then followed Cameron outside. At sight of Many-Horses she made a trilling sound and sank down at his side. He smiled and said, "No *Apachu* . . . Navajo."

While Cameron made strips of cloth, White Magpie used her talon-like hands to tear clothing aside. Because the light was poor, she put her face very close, sat back, and told the cowman they would have to remove the old Indian's shirt. The bullet had cut across his stomach. As they worked, Cameron said Many-Horses needed whiskey. The old bronco replied in a firm but tired-sounding voice: "No whiskey!"

They had his upper body exposed when they heard two gunshots southeast in the timber. They paid no attention as White Magpie eased Many-Horses forward to wrap him. He gasped. "Too tight."

They ignored that, finished the wrapping, and Cameron stood up, too quickly. He had to unkink one knee before returning inside where the sound of crying diverted him, but only for a moment. He dragged one of the bunks outside, told White Magpie to find blankets, and, the moment she was inside, Cameron got both arms under Many-Horses, straining to lift the

Indian and put him on the bunk. The bandage in front was soggy red, and Cameron's leg almost crumpled.

White Magpie returned with two blankets and the whiskey bottle. While Cameron supported the old Indian, White Magpie forced the bottle's spout past Many-Horses's clenched teeth and trickled whiskey until he had to swallow or gag. He swallowed.

White Magpie went back inside. As Cameron worked to stop the bleeding, he could hear the old woman crooning in a language he did not understand. When she eventually came back, she had Yellow Bluebell with her. The girl's face was streaked with tears. She had been terrified so long she was unable to speak. She was clutching the mouse nest to her chest.

Out in the meadow the old buffalo cow made lowing sounds. Only Many-Horses listened and rolled his head to the right. White Magpie and the cowman made a fresh bandage to replace the soaked one. Again they had to turn the Indian to complete the wrapping.

When they had finished, Cameron stood looking down as he said: "Could have been worse. It could have gone through him."

The old cowman tipped the bottle, swallowed, and handed it to the old woman. She trickled whiskey over the outer cloth of the new bandage. That made Many-Horses react with more strength than he had shown before.

White Magpie went back inside, found two candles, and lighted them. The smoke had dissipated, but its smell lingered. Otherwise the place had been devastated. True to female instinct the old woman began making order out of chaos, as best she could. She called Yellow Bluebell to come and help.

Night was settling. Andrew Cameron came inside to help. The more he worked, the more his almost lipless mouth became fixed in a bloodless slit. He eventually went out and away to see if his horse was still out there. It was. He returned to the cabin, yanked one of those chairs that exuded resin beside Many-Horses's bunk, fired up his pipe, and was wondering the same thing when the Indian said: "Sam gone long time."

Cameron said nothing, but, after resting a while, he arose, went out to get his horse, led it back, saddled up without a word, paused before mounting to spin the cylinder of his six-gun, and lever the saddle gun. Only the hand gun needed reloading. As he punched out spent casings and plugged in replacements, he called to White Magpie. When she appeared in the doorway, he told her he would bring back medicine, that he would try to find Sam, and got a-horse-back as he also said: "Keep the girl working. Keep her mind off things."

They watched him head up the easterly rise on a southerly angle.

Many-Horses hadn't eaten in hours. The whiskey loosened him, and he slept. Yellow Bluebell wanted to know how badly he was hurt. White Magpie employed her innate capacity for prevarication, making a deprecatory gesture and telling Belle she had seen men hurt as badly, and they had not even got off their horses.

She went to her cooking hole, got a stingy fire going, and made stew for herself and the girl. Neither of them was hungry, but the old woman had used the traditional ruse of all females when there was unpleasantness — she cooked a meal. She had done it for more years than she could recall.

Yellow Bluebell succumbed to the letdown which invariably followed periods of horror and fear. She went back to her dark corner to feed her mice pine nuts until she fell asleep.

The old woman let her fire die to coals. She hoped there would be coals under the ash come morning. She went over to the chair beside Many-Horses's bunk, sat down, and softly called to him: "Apache . . . Apache."

He opened his eyes and regarded her. For some time he had come to the belief that she called him that because she knew it annoyed him. He looked at her and said: "Crow White Magpie."

She bristled. "Lakota!" she barked at him.

Many-Horses smiled. "Crow woman same as me Apache. I call you Crow woman."

White Magpie gazed steadily at the Navajo for a long time before inclining her head. "You Navajo. Old Navajo."

He tried to nod. "You old Lakota woman."

White Magpie raised a hand to cover her nearly toothless mouth as she laughed. Many-Horses smiled and fell asleep.

In the wee hours Many-Horses awakened White Magpie. "Where is Sam?"

She said: "Go to sleep."

"By now he should come back. Maybe he got shot. Maybe someone should look for him."

The old woman sounded exasperated when she replied: "He didn't get shot. Wait for morning."

"I go find him."

"You don't stand up. You die standin' up. You run out of blood. I give you more whiskey."

"No!"

"Then go to sleep!"

By the light of a new day the degree of devastation, even after efforts to put things back in order, was demoralizing. As the old woman stirred her cooking hole to life, she called to Many-Horses and got no answer. She went around to the bunk. The old man was gray and motionless. She put her cheek to his nostrils. He was breathing but shallowly. She sat beside him until Yellow Bluebell came out on her way to the creek to wash. She had the soft, fuzzy nest in her hands. White Magpie watched her go, saw the buffalo cow and her calf also watching.

The sun eventually got high enough to cast light and warmth into the meadow. White Magpie stopped using the chair and sat on the ground beside the old man's bunk. Once she arose to raise the blankets very carefully. There was blood on the underside of the blankets and also on the bandage. As she was lowering the blankets, Many-Horses said: "*Buenas días.*"

She considered his face with obvious suspicion. "What does that mean?"

His dark eyes with their muddy whites showed a teasing spark. "I don't know. I think it means you are a handsome woman. Something like that."

She called him a name in Lakota. He nodded. "What does that mean?"

"It means you are a liar."

The light in his eyes faded.

She said, "I have broth for you."

He closed his eyes.

When Yellow Bluebell returned from the creek with shiny cheeks, she stood beside the bunk, looking down as she asked a question in Crow. White Magpie replied in English. "No. He live long time. Apache tough men. There is broth on the table."

"Where is the skinny old tall one?"

"His name is Sam. Remember that. I don't know where he is."

"Maybe he don't come back."

White Magpie gently pushed aside a loose strand of the girl's hair. "Maybe he don't," she replied and swiftly added: "Maybe he do."

The old woman held the golden necklace in her fingers and told Yellow Bluebell in Crow that, like her people, like the Crow people, like even the Apache people, there were good ones and bad ones. She tucked the necklace inside the girl's dress and said: "Good white-eyes too. We have two."

The old cow bellowed anxiously at her calf who was racing in huge circles with its tail over his back. Both women watched. The girl smiled slightly which White Magpie noticed and said: "Go eat."

As Yellow Bluebell departed, Many-Horses said: "Talk to her only in English."

White Magpie looked down. His eyes were sunken but bright. "I do that every day."

"Not now you don't," Many-Horses said, sounding peevish.

"I'll bring the broth."

"And a spoon," he muttered.

"No, I lift and pour, an' you swallow."

When she returned with a bowl, he would have tried to push himself up, but she put a hand on his chest, pushing him back down. She slid a skinny arm under his shoulders and lifted. At the same time she raised the bowl. He swallowed once, tentatively, then drank the bowl empty. As she eased him down, he said: "Sam in trouble."

She shook her head. "Not as much as you. He will come."

"Do you know what he called me?"

"Old bastard, an' you thought it was his name for you."

"No! I know what it means. Almost like in Mexican. They say *bastardo*."

"Many days he don't call you that. Go to sleep."

"I got to find him. Mexicans have a word for it . . . *compañero*. It means . . . better than friend."

She put the bowl aside and perched on the arm of the chair. "If you don't sleep, I pour whiskey down you."

He closed his eyes and kept them closed until she was in the cabin. Then he opened them. In his own

138

language he muttered something about men not needing biting dogs, bucking horses, or women who talk back.

CHAPTER
ELEVEN

A Long Night

Two days passed. Sam did not return, and Many-Horses got weaker by the day. Twice he tried to leave the bed. Each time he did that, White Magpie appeared without a sound, scolded, pushed him down, and rearranged the blankets — partly because he had pushed half of them off the bed, partly to see their undersides. There was fresh blood.

She thought of climbing to the roof to repair the hole where the rangeman had climbed out and escaped. Once she even went to ask Many-Horses how it was done. He was asleep.

If she worried, she kept it from Yellow Bluebell, who had her own problem. The mother mouse would leave the nest for long periods. The last time she returned without her baby, which was now as large and much heavier than she was.

Yellow Bluebell sensed the mother mouse wanted her baby to leave the nest. She mentioned this to White Magpie, who answered without facing the girl: "The time comes." She turned and smiled.

The mother mouse did not seem to miss her baby. From the way she rearranged the nest, so that she alone could enjoy it with no crowding, told Yellow Bluebell that White Magpie was right. It had been time.

She went to the creek to fetch water, and the buffalo calf feinted her, tail up, head low. She laughed. The old cow watched with mild concern. Belle caught the calf by the neck. It struggled briefly, then stood like a dog while she picked off ticks and scratched its back.

When she got back, a tired, head-hung horse was standing near Many-Horses's bunk. She hesitated. She had not seen the horse before. She put the bucket of water near the door and fled.

Sam, who carried a minimum of weight, looked gaunt as he and the old woman talked at the table. He had dried blood on one cheek in the matting of a scruffy beard. She said: "He got away?"

"On foot. I found his horse an' waited for him to come to get it. He never come."

White Magpie said: "Smelled you."

"Somethin'. I waited all night an' the next day."

"You wait, an' he walk."

Sam nodded. "Is the whiskey bottle broke?"

She got it. It hadn't been broken but was only half full. As he held it aloft, she said: "Many-Horses's medicine."

He drank, pushed the bottle away, and turned on the bench to look out where the bed was.

White Magpie said: "Blood no stop."

Sam leaned far backwards to ease the pain in his back.

The old woman arose. "I cook for you."

He tiredly smiled, took the bottle, and went out to Many-Horses. The old Indian faintly brightened. He said he must have been asleep. He hadn't heard Sam come. He also said he slept a lot and held out an unsteady hand for the bottle. Sam helped him swallow three times then stood up, holding the bottle, waiting for the effect, which normally required time. Not with Many-Horses. Color came under the dark hide. The eyes with their muddy whites brightened. He said: "You catch him?"

Sam retold what he had explained to White Magpie. Many-Horses listened in silence. After a while he spoke in a strong voice, the voice Sam was accustomed to hearing. "Too bad you no kill him."

Sam perched on the arm of a chair. "Scairt the whey out of him, partner. I don't figure he'll come back."

Many-Horses's gaze did not leave Sam's face. He did not say a word. Sam let him have two more swallows from the bottle, and Many-Horses closed his eyes.

White Magpie came out, took the bottle, and went around to the cooking hole where she was making a kettle full of bear stew. Yellow Bluebell came out, glanced timidly at Sam, and he smiled at her.

"How is Missus Mouse?" he asked.

She smiled and came a little closer. He noticed something that shocked him. The pretty dress with its red ribbons no longer hung on her. Because he did not know what to say, he went over to off-saddle the horse, bearing a left shoulder brand whose design was a connected A C in a circle.

142

He hobbled the animal out in the meadow. It fought him to get its head down. The cow and her calf stood like statues, watching. The horse was tucked up. He hardly more than spared a look at the buffalo.

Sam brought the bridle, blanket, and saddle back, slung over one shoulder. He dumped them along the front wall, and went inside when the old woman called to him in her high-pitched voice.

He emptied two bowls of stew, kicked out of his boots, and, on his way to the bunk, shed his shell belt and holstered sidearm.

Many-Horses slept the balance of that day and until sunrise the next morning. White Magpie had difficulty getting him to eat. Sam returned from the creek, carrying the water bucket Yellow Bluebell usually filled. She walked beside him now, looking at the ground. He asked about the mouse. She told him, and he told her essentially the same thing White Magpie had told her. He handed her the bucket to be taken inside and went to stand beside the old Navajo's bed. If Many-Horses recognized him or even knew he was standing there, he gave no sign of it.

Sam took the peach tin out to grease the buffalo cow's wounds, which were nearly healed. She watched him approach, stood her ground until the last minute, then bunted the calf, and moved away. He tried three times to get close and twice she sidled. The third time she did not move, but her mouth was open with the tongue curled back. Sam slathered her scabs and scratched her forehead where the hair was thick, curly, and black. She continued to roll her tongue back with her mouth open but made no warning sounds.

When he got back to the cabin, the old woman was waiting. She held aloft a skinny arm. "Two men," she said, indicating the easterly uplands, and dropped her arm.

Sam squinted up there, without seeing anything.

The old woman added: "One big, hairy face."

Sam remained in plain sight after White Magpie had gone around to her cooking hole. Many-Horses made a grating sound. When Sam looked down, the old Indian looked directly at him and on through as he mumbled words in a language Sam did not understand.

He got his rifle to go up the easterly slope. White Magpie stopped him. "They see horse out there. They see you, too. They wait when you come." She raised both wrinkled old arms into the position of someone aiming a gun, lowered her arms, tapped Sam hard in the middle of the chest with a rigid finger, and said: "You."

Sam started up the hill with the agitated old woman watching. She went back and berated Many-Horses for Sam's recklessness. She told him those riders had wanted him to see them. She said they were going to kill him.

Many-Horses faintly frowned. A rasping voice had entered his increasing world of shadows. He growled something the old woman did not understand and closed his eyes.

She found Yellow Bluebell in her dark corner and told her to go southward and hide. The girl watched round-eyed as the old woman took Many-Horses's new carbine and disappeared around the side of the cabin.

The mouse chose this moment to scamper up the wall to the rafters and would not be coaxed down by pine nuts. She sat up there, vigorously washing her face. Yellow Bluebell went to the door and peered out. There was no sign of White Magpie. Many-Horses twisted feebly under his blankets and began singing.

Yellow Bluebell went back for her mouse, who was no longer in sight except for the tip of her long tail, still flipping about inside the hole in the roof. The girl stood still, listening. There was nothing to be heard. She returned to the doorway, watched for movement in all directions, but even the fractious buffalo calf was curled up, asleep in front of his mother.

She approached Many-Horses's bed. The old man was sweating and shivering. It was a hot morning. She wanted to get him some water. Instead, she did as White Magpie had said: she angled southward up the slope into the trees, paused once to look behind her and listen, then struck out southward. She had never been very far in that direction. Fear gripped her heart with every step.

She went almost two miles, then balked at going any farther. No one could find her, particularly rangemen on horses. She barely left sign. She did not weigh enough for that. She reversed her course, got close enough to be able to see the meadow and the house, sat down with her knees drawn up and encircled by both arms, and, while listening for sounds in her vicinity, watched the meadow and the cabin.

Yellow Bluebell was an Indian. She possessed the endless patience of her people. Even after the sun was low, she did not move. Just before dusk she saw White Magpie. The old woman moved cat-like among huge trees, carrying Many-Horses's Winchester.

Yellow Bluebell watched without arising. There was an occasional wisp of a shadow behind her. Not until they both passed through one of those cathedral-like downward spears of sunlight did she recognize Sam. Then she stood up.

She arrived at the cabin with dusk coming, passed Many-Horses's bed, and peeked inside. Sam and White Magpie were talking. She sounded irritated. He said very little. When Sam glanced doorward and saw the girl, he interrupted the old woman's tirade. White Magpie whirled, then made a little sound, and rushed to enclose the girl in both arms, crooning in that language Sam did not understand.

White Magpie abruptly pushed Yellow Bluebell to arm's length to scold her for not doing as she had been told, flee southward. Yellow Bluebell surprised Sam. She shook free of the old woman's hands and answered her in English. "I do like you say. I run so far until I wanted to sit. So I came back to see house and wait."

She flung past the old woman, who stood in obvious surprise, and went to her dark corner, looking for her mother mouse.

Sam held the bottle to thin daylight, before taking two swallows. This time, instead of putting it back on the shelf, he put it under a blanket on his bed. White Magpie watched and said: "Many-Horses's medicine."

He looked at the old woman without speaking.

She went out to the cooking hole, used two sticks of fat wood to light coals, and muttered to herself as she got the iron kettle where she wanted it. She looked up when Yellow Bluebell appeared nearby, timid and expressionless. The old woman started speaking in Crow, heard Many-Horses groan, and switched to English.

"I worry. I got no more than you. Bring wood."

When the girl returned, they smiled at each other, the old woman's sharp words forgotten. White Magpie said: "No find 'em. Sam say they hide. Come in the night."

Yellow Bluebell fingered her necklace with its gold emblem, and the old woman nodded. "Good medicine?"

The girl smiled back. "It is mine."

The old woman's smile faded. She turned back to stirring the fire. "People say they own things. I think things own people."

Sam came around the side of the cabin, carrying his rifle. Before looking at the crouching women, he stood a long time gazing past the pair of buffalo to the far rim of timber.

White Magpie said: "Not enough dark yet."

Sam hunkered, leaning with both hands on the rifle. "I'm hopin' they try to steal the horse."

White Magpie sniffed. "They got other horse," and held up a rack of thoroughly recooked rib bones. The aroma made Sam forget her innuendo.

He returned to the house with the women. Many-Horses was talking clearly for a change. "Blood moon come now."

White Magpie paused to look upwards over her shoulder. She entered the cabin with her lips sucked flat.

Sam hadn't eaten since morning. He was hungry enough to strip rib bones down to hard whiteness. Yellow Bluebell ate solemnly. She knew White Magpie's different expressions. The old woman ate sparingly, her lips flat and her eyes smoldering.

When night came, they lighted one candle. Sam thought they should light two. The old woman shook her head. It wasn't important enough to argue over.

Sam went outside to fire up his pipe and tip his face like an animal, seeking scent. Many-Horses was motionless. Sam stood beside the bed a long time. When White Magpie came out, she, too, stood in silence. She said: "In the morning," and brushed Sam's sleeve to interrupt his reverie.

This time they took Yellow Bluebell with them up the slope and into the dark forest. She asked no questions and neither of her companions spoke.

Where the old woman squatted with Many-Horses's gun, she sat like a stone, eyes fixed on the heavens. Sam, who was accustomed to her moods, sat beside the girl. When he spoke, it was in a loud enough whisper for her to hear every word, whether she understood them all or not.

148

"She thinks they come back to find my cache of yellow dirt. Maybe. For a fact, it makes men act crazy."

"You think they come?"

He shifted on fir needles before replying. "They're crazy if they do. That scrawny one we caught . . . I think he got the hell scairt out of him." Sam leaned back to ease the pain and said no more.

They sat while the moon arose. It was pinkish red, very close to being full. In the westerly distance a pack of coursing wolves paused to howl at it, and White Magpie shivered, which her companions did not notice. During their wait for the horsemen Sam told White Magpie he thought the scrawny one they had captured believed his lie about the origin of the gold his furry-faced partner had found in the cowman's saddlebags.

White Magpie had more immediate concerns. "No talk," she said, and they became silent.

The old woman crept close to the final tier of huge old trees, got belly down with the Winchester, shoved forward. Sam and Yellow Bluebell did the same. The girl brushed close to Sam several times. He smiled at her.

She drew the necklace from inside her dress and held it for Sam's inspection. He had seen it before and whispered that he thought it was very handsome.

White Magpie hissed at them. "You don't see in dark! You don't see in sunlight!" She reached past Sam to hold the necklace briefly. "What is made on front?"

Yellow Bluebell answered in a whisper. "Little bird on tree."

The old woman checked her rising irritation when she replied. "No! White bird!" she said, and pushed the necklace back into its warm place.

The wolves had coursed on around from the west to the north. When they sounded from that direction, White Magpie listened intently, then squirmed around to peer into the rearward darkness. If the wolves hadn't caught horse and man scent in the west, and now had not detected it northward, the night-stalking horsemen had to be coming from the east or the south.

Sam leaned to tell her this when she reached with a claw-like hand to silence him. She whispered: "I know."

Sam led the retreat. When the old woman would have pushed in front, he caught her by the arm and pushed her back. She did not make another effort to take the lead.

They moved like ghosts. Sam did not believe they could be seen. Their periods of exposure were no more than thirty feet, from one forest giant to the next. And it was dark.

When he thought they had traveled easterly far enough, he halted. White Magpie did not speak. She simply nodded her head as though she had read his mind, which she hadn't done. It was obvious that, if the night stalkers were approaching from the east, it would have been apparent by now.

Sam struck out southward but on a westering angle. He wanted to be able to see the cabin and the meadow, something the rangemen would also want to have in sight.

A bobcat, sleeping overhead on a broad fir limb, was startled out of its slumber and sprang up, as the scent below reached it, and lost its balance. When it hit the ground, it snarled and fled. White Magpie was raising the Winchester when Sam knocked it aside. He did not say a word. Neither did the old woman.

They continued on their angling course. The falling bobcat had frightened Yellow Bluebell so badly she walked as closely to Sam as she could, without stepping on his heels.

Occasionally they could see out, could see patches of the meadow. At those times White Magpie looked steadily at the moon. The higher it went, the less was its reddish tint.

Sam eventually stopped to listen. The woman heard it, too — riders approaching at a slow walk.

Sam stood motionless for as long as was necessary for him to determine the course of the riders, then went wraith-like among the easterly trees. It was possible to see the cabin and the meadow. As they watched, the buffalo cow lumbered heavily to her feet, facing southeasterly. Sam had often heard that buffalo could detect scent a mile. As he watched the cow, he thought it was probably true. There was nothing else to hold her attention in that direction.

White Magpie brushed his sleeve. "There," she whispered and jutted her jaw in the same direction — southeasterly.

Sam heard nothing until a steel horseshoe grated over stone. As a sound it was almost indiscernible. He waited for the sound again but did not hear it.

White Magpie stepped past Sam, head high. She signaled him to come to her and said: "Many-Horses."

He did not hear it until she was silent, and he had to strain to hear it then.

White Magpie said: "Death song."

The sound of slow-pacing horses seemed closer. Sam gestured for the old woman to go back with Yellow Bluebell. Unless the riders changed course, they were going to pass Sam's tree within easy carbine range. If they passed farther to the west, perhaps along the rim overlooking the cabin and meadow, because Sam carried a long gun, a rifle, they would still be within his range.

The riders stopped. Sam got down low to the ground and peeked around the tree. He could see neither the men nor their horses. He looked for the old woman and the girl and failed to find them, either, which did not surprise him. White Magpie's people had been making themselves invisible for centuries.

A man's coarse voice came clearly, even though its owner was keeping it low. The words were distinguishable in the relative silence. "You hear the old tomahawk?"

"Yeah. I thought he was dead."

"If he's awake so are the others."

The growl of a voice ended this conversation when it said: "Won't make a damn' difference, Jed. We'll do like

152

they done. Ain't no winders. Only when we kick the door open, we'll be shootin'."

Sam did not hear the squeak of leather as the men remounted, but he heard the horses resume their slow-paced advance.

CHAPTER TWELVE

A Wasted Vigil

White Magpie was sitting, twisted half around. If she had heard the rangemen, she gave no indication of it. She was rigid, and her head was tilted. Eventually, sure of what she had heard, she got close to Sam and whispered: "Rider coming from south."

Sam cocked his head but heard nothing. The old woman gripped his arm. "Three. Not two . . . three."

That made a difference. He gestured for the women to follow and padded soundlessly southward. White Magpie followed but with powerful doubts. Sam was taking them in the direction of the night riders, but he changed course, heading eastward, and that made even less sense to the old woman, but she followed with Yellow Bluebell on her heels.

Where Sam halted, the sound of a single approaching horse was clearly audible. The animal seemed to have been following the old cowman's trail, until it branched off and came in Sam's direction.

He told the women to hide and be quiet, which they both did. Sam selected the right tree for his purpose, got into position on its westerly side, took a strong handhold on the rough bark, and gently placed the rifle over his forearm.

But there was an abrupt interruption before he even saw the horsemen. A man let go with an astonished squawk. It was followed by a bellow of hair-raising profanity and three gunshots as fast as someone could drop the hammer of a six-gun with the trigger held fully back.

Sam grounded his weapon. Behind him a sharp voice said: "They running."

It was true. The sound of fleeing horsemen was audible, and Sam had an errant thought. Regardless of the circumstances he would never race a horse in darkness through a thick forest, but clearly everyone did not feel the same.

He listened until the sounds of flight faded, and somewhere southeasterly a rider resumed his way without haste. Yellow Bluebell saw him first and gripped Sam's sleeve as she jutted her jaw. The rider was working his way among the trees. He was a massive wraith and so was his horse.

White Magpie spoke loudly. "You good man."

The bulky wraith stopped dead still. He turned his head from side to side before speaking. "What are you doin' up here, old woman?"

She answered in the same strident voice. "Wait for you."

Andrew Cameron snorted, squeezed his horse, and would have ridden past them if the old woman had not stepped directly in front of the big sorrel horse.

Cameron leaned both hands atop the horn and scowled downward as Sam came into sight. The last to come was Yellow Bluebell. She had been terrified for several hours, and the big old man, wearing a sheep pelt coat astride one of the largest horses she had ever seen, was like something out of Crow myths — a terrifying warrior of the night.

Cameron led the way. The others followed. When they reached the rim, he put one hand on the cantle and twisted to look back as he said: "Where's the old bronco?"

Sam answered. "Down yonder, not doin' good."

Cameron sat forward and rattled the reins as he started down the slope. "I got medicine," he growled, and said no more until they reached the cabin where he dismounted, braced a moment on the saddle before placing weight on one leg, dropped the reins, and went to stand beside the bed.

On a dark night, dressed as he was, the cowman looked almost as large as a bear. Yellow Bluebell would not go near him. He leaned to speak softly. "I brought medicine."

To White Magpie's surprise Many-Horses answered. "Who shoot?"

Cameron remained bent when he replied. "I couldn't see 'em well, but I expect I know. They come toward me. One drew his gun. I shot three times. They tucked tail like rabbits." Cameron did for him an unusual thing. He placed a gnarled, callused hand on the old Indian's shoulder. "We can talk tomorrow."

"You shoot 'em?" Many-Horses asked.

Cameron answered gruffly. "Too dark. I don't think so, but they didn't shoot me."

As they entered the house, where the old woman lighted another of their precious candles, Yellow Bluebell remained outside. Many-Horses felt for the girl's hand and gripped it. "Send old woman," he said and released her fingers. She went as far as the door where shadowy candlelight made the large old man in the heavy coat cast frightening shadows that moved. She went around where dying coals from the cooking hole gave warmth.

Sam told the cowman about the ruse he had used to convince the scrawny captive the nugget his partner had found in Cameron's saddlebags came from an old mine southeast of Boulder, and, before Sam had finished, Cameron felt for a bench and sat down with one leg pushed straight out as he wagged his head and growled a reply. "It didn't work. If it had, they wouldn't have come back up here." He leaned to rub the leg. "They know I come up here. They know my trail. The hefty one ain't dumb."

White Magpie brought the bottle. Both men drank and gradually brightened a little. Cameron watched the old woman reach for the bottle and said: " 'Nother one in my saddlebags, along with the medicine." He paused, looking tiredly into the candlelight. "The bleedin' don't stop?"

Sam shook his head. "But it's down to a trickle."

Cameron turned to face Sam. "When it's down to a trickle, there ain't much left." He looked at the old woman who shook her head.

Yellow Bluebell, now having gained the courage to enter, sidled around against the wall to reach her dark corner where she huddled as quiet as her pet mouse.

Cameron took another pull on the bottle, handed it to the old woman, and addressed Sam. "Break the buffalo calf to lead," he said, and left them to care for his horse and return with his saddlebags slung over a shoulder. He spoke as though he hadn't left. "I don't know about buffalo, but with cattle, if the calf s broke to lead, the cow'll follow."

He and Sam went back out into the night, where a chill was setting in. Cameron gazed at the bed where Many-Horses's shallow breathing was audible. "Well, he's old. The medicine I brought can't stop bleedin'. I'm sorry. He was a good Injun. Mostly folks in his shape die between two an' four in the mornin'." Cameron ranged a glance up the sidehill, and his voice was hard. "I'll get those sons of bitches. They come back to work for me three years straight runnin'. They wasn't the best, but after a while they got to know the range an' how I wanted things done."

White Magpie appeared in the doorway with candlelight limning her. They went back inside where she had set the table with two tin plates of cold stew.

They sat down. The cowman did not eat much, but Sam did. In the dark corner, where visibility was poor, someone giggled. White Magpie clarified: "Mouse come home."

Cameron refused Sam's offer of a bunk, rolled into a blanket without removing anything but his shell belt

158

and gun, punched his hat to make a pillow, and was asleep before the old woman snuffed out the candles.

White Magpie had been a lifelong light sleeper and was stirring before sunrise. The moon was gone. The sun wouldn't arrive for another two or three hours. She used fat wood and dry grass to build a fire in the cooking hole.

Many-Horses spoke her name. She went to him. His gaze was discernibly stronger as was his voice when he said: "Get small rocks."

She nodded but could not find very many until false dawn came, then she brought back two armloads, and dropped them beside the bed. Many-Horses said: "Help me sit up."

She shook her head. "Tell me what you want."

He feebly gestured. "Make circle."

She squatted to obey, expressionless and silent. Many-Horses feebly struggled to lie on his side and watch. When she had finished, he said: "Close circle." She pushed stones until they touched, then sat solemnly, regarding his wasted face. He continued to lie on his side until the old woman stood up. He tried to chant, but there were no words, and the song was broken at intervals until he gathered the strength to continue. Someone inside moaned in his sleep, which diverted her attention. Many-Horses didn't make a sound, but he fell down face forward with one hand and arm over the edge of the bunk. It swung once, scattering stones.

Dawn was breaking when Sam and Cameron were awakened by an eerie trilling. When they got outside, the old woman was sitting in pale light, looking at the dark, old relaxed hand and the broken circle of stones, rocking slightly as she sang.

The old cowman limped to the side of the bed. When Sam came up, he said: "We'll take turns with the shovel."

Sam bent to touch Many-Horses. White Magpie stopped her chant and struck his hand away. "No feel," she said. "White man no touch."

Sam straightened up as the old cowman said: "It's bad for his spirit if a white man touches a dead Injun."

It would not occur to Sam for several days to wonder how Andrew Cameron knew such a thing.

They worked at making the grave until the sun was high, something else of which White Magpie did not approve, but there was no other way. To make a burial platform they would need tall young trees, and there were only large trees.

There was no talk as they dug, and Cameron had to sit often with one leg shoved out. Sam used those respites to lie flat out until the pain in his back lessened.

White Magpie rolled Many-Horses in his bloody blankets and scolded him for leaving. Yellow Bluebell watched round-eyed from the doorway with the mouse on her shoulder near her ear.

The men carried Many-Horses to the hole, got down on their knees to lower him gently. As Cameron arose,

160

he told White Magpie to fetch Many-Horses's new guns. When she brought them, Cameron placed them beside the blanket bundle, then had to rest.

Sam jerked his head at the old woman and, without speaking, curled one hand and held it briefly to his mouth. White Magpie went inside the cabin with Yellow Bluebell at her side, and the old woman spoke softly to her in Crow, after which Yellow Bluebell went to her dark place and cried.

By the time they had tamped and covered the grave, both men needed whiskey. When the first bottle the old man had brought was empty, Cameron told her to fetch the bottle from his saddlebags, which she did. When the men weren't watching, she cupped a hand, poured whiskey into it, and trickled it over the grave with her lips moving.

Cameron returned to the cabin long enough to eat cooked, spiced bear meat, then went outside to study the easterly forest. When Sam joined him, he said: "I'm goin' back. If they're down there, I'll kill 'em."

"Need company?" Sam asked and got a black scowl but no reply as the cowman pitched his saddlebags against the wall near the door and went to fetch his horse. As Sam watched, he told himself, if the renegade rangemen were watching, they would see the cowman leave the uplands. He doubted that they would shoot him. They would do better not to. His killing would arouse the countryside, and that is exactly what they did not need — aroused folks, poking and prying.

When he looked westerly, Yellow Bluebell with a coiled rope over one shoulder and carrying the peach tin of grease was walking toward the old cow and her calf.

He went inside where White Magpie was hunched at the table, both shriveled hands clasped. She did not raise her eyes until he spoke. "Tonight we bed down in the forest."

She did not speak but turned her head to gaze past the open door in the direction of the circle of stones. She arose and went around to her cooking hole. She was busy there until she heard the buffalo bellow and twisted around to look.

Sam also heard and came to the doorway. Yellow Bluebell's initial attempt to break the calf to lead was a failure. The calf weighed more than she did, and, although she hung on for dear life, the calf dragged her in the direction of its upset mother.

She lost her grip. The calf dragged the rope, whirled to look back as the cow dropped her head, and pawed. Sam held his breath, so did White Magpie. But the calf nuzzled enough to divert the cow, and she did not charge.

Sam met Yellow Bluebell coming back. One of the red ribbons had been torn off her dress. She clutched it in one hand, tears brimming when Sam came up. He walked as far as the cooking hole with her, then told White Magpie to explain how animals were broke to lead.

They hid in the forest after nightfall. Sam and the old woman went back to be close enough to watch the cabin. As that red moon climbed, it became silver, and in an eerie way visibility was excellent.

Sam chewed bear jerky. The old woman did not eat. They had left Yellow Bluebell under a mound of needles with orders to hunker down and not move, which she obeyed. Hours passed during which they alternately watched the cabin and the moon which steadily sank, leaving behind more cold than they had felt in months.

When dawn came, Sam nudged the old woman. They went back for Yellow Bluebell and cautiously worked their way to the house, using shadows wherever they found them, and got a surprise. There was a single set of boot prints. Tracks led completely around the cabin. The door hung open, but the tracks did not go inside. They showed signs of shuffling at the grave, then went southward a fair distance, and cut up the slope into the timber.

Sam told the old woman one man moving carefully could have escaped their vigil, particularly since he had been on foot. She neither agreed nor disagreed, but obviously that was what had happened. One of the trespassers had eluded detection. Sam thought it would be the one named Carville because the prints were small and had made slight impressions.

White Magpie worried a cooking fire from layers of ash. Sam went inside to nap, and, while lying there, considered the medicine Andrew Cameron had brought. One blue bottle intrigued him. He arose to pick it up. The handwritten label said: **Laudanum**. He replaced it atop the table and returned to the bunk. He slept most of the day and might have slept longer except for the old woman, plucking at his sleeve. She had a bowl of hot stew.

As Sam moved to the table to eat, the old woman went to stand in the doorway. Over there she made a cackling laugh. Sam took his bowl to the doorway.

Yellow Bluebell was feeding the calf as much rolled barley as she had scraped up. The calf ate, and perhaps the scent brought the buffalo cow, but the girl got between them until the calf had lipped it all up. She scratched the old cow with one hand and scratched the calf with the other hand. As she did this, she eased the rope off the calf. Sam chuckled.

White Magpie said: "No more grain," and went around to her cooking hole. When the girl came up, the old woman spoke to her in Crow. Yellow Bluebell smiled shyly at Sam, left the rope inside, and went around the edge of the meadow, gathering whatever it was the old woman had told her to gather.

Sam was restless. For all he knew those rangemen had ridden up the creek to the waterfall. He would have taken his rifle and gone up there if the old woman hadn't made her keening sound. The old cowman was coming down the slope astride his sorrel horse.

Sam waited until Cameron could hear him, then explained about the tracks made in the night. Cameron rode on up, dismounted, and tossed a small, light sack to the ground. "For the girl . . . what's her name?"

"Belle."

"For her to chum that calf with."

Cameron off-saddled, favored his leg, and sank down on the bench. "Grover'n Carville come back last night, cleaned out their gatherings from the bunkhouse, an' left. They waited until no one was around." Cameron stuffed and lighted his pipe as he put a shrewd gaze on Sam Sloan. "They left tracks goin' toward Boulder. Because I had a score to settle, I followed. They went half way then cut straight north."

Cameron had to pause to relight the pipe, and Sam said: "Back up here?"

Cameron puffed briefly as he nodded his head. Then he almost smiled at Sam. "They never worked this hard for me."

Sam almost smiled, too, when he replied: "Your cattle ain't gold."

White Magpie opened the light sack and called Yellow Bluebell, told her in Crow to go visit the calf with rolled barley, which the girl did but not until she got the water bucket in order to carry the grain.

The three adults watched. The calf came, attracted by the scent, but so did its mother, and this time getting between them wasn't enough. The cow pushed the girl aside, using just her head. Yellow Bluebell poured feed in the grass in one place and fed the calf in another place.

Cameron chuckled. He was sucking on a cold pipe and did not notice. They told him about Yellow Bluebell's attempt with the rope. This time he did not make a sound, just watched the girl and animals in the meadow.

Eventually he knocked out the dottle and told Sam to help her break the calf to lead because autumn wasn't far off.

White Magpie went to the cabin and returned with the full bottle which she handed to the old cowman. He held it a long time while he looked at her. After taking two pulls and passing the bottle to Sam, he said: "Old woman, I want you to take a walk with me."

She nodded, without speaking, and went around to her cooking hole. When Yellow Bluebell returned with the empty bucket, the old cowman told her not to take so much or she'd run out before she'd taught the calf to lead. He then arose, ignored Sam and the girl to go around where the old woman was holding a claw-like hand in front of her face as a shield from the heat. He hunkered down beside her. She looked once, then went back to cooking. Andrew Cameron said: "After supper we walk."

The old woman put a pair of shrewd black eyes on the cowman and bobbed her head up and down, bird fashion.

They ate mostly in silence. White Magpie had lighted two candles, to which Sam said nothing although he thought one would have been enough. They only had seven candles.

When they were finished, and the cowman reached for the bottle, the old woman said: "No!" in so explosive a manner Cameron's arm hung briefly in air before he pulled it back, arose, and jerked his head.

White Magpie followed him out into the warm, dying late afternoon.

CHAPTER
THIRTEEN

Impending Changes

Sam watched them walk out into the meadow and turned to squint up the easterly slope. The cowman said Grover and Carville had headed back toward the highlands. If they had, then, for a fact, they would be somewhere, probably watching the cabin and the meadow. Enough daylight still remained to see clearly.

Andrew Cameron had left his sheep-pelt rider's coat behind, but he was still a thick, wide, slow-moving figure. Sam had to fall back on his earlier supposition that they would not shoot the cowman, but, as he stood watching the hulking old man and the shriveled, bird-like old woman, it troubled him that Cameron made such an excellent target.

While Sam watched, the cowman and White Magpie stopped near the creek and sat down. This diminished their visibility, and Sam had a reassuring thought — they were well beyond accurate saddle-gun range.

Cameron pulled a stalk of wild oats and chewed it. White Magpie waited. Cameron briefly watched the buffalo and her calf, spat out the grass, and looked from beneath tufted eyebrows as he said: "There's a white bird . . . ?"

The old woman nodded. "Come to me twice."

"Well, I never told folks . . . mebbe one or two at most . . . but once I seen a white bird." He plucked another stalk and chewed it, gazing solemnly at her.

She asked what it had told him. He spat out the second stalk and looked annoyed. "I don't put no store by that kind of thing."

"What did it *tell* you?"

He squirmed on the ground before answering. "It was my leg. Sometimes it gives me hell, mostly at night. Sometimes I don't sleep good. I commenced to get out of bed to fetch some whiskey when the damned leg folded up under me. I had a time of it, just gettin' back into bed."

The old woman said nothing. She sat waiting.

"I was tryin' to sleep. Maybe I was asleep. I saw a white bird, big almost as a chicken. It spoke." He paused to pluck another length of grass but, as he continued, threw it aside. "It was a bad dream. I must have dozed off. Next mornin' I could still hear it. It said an old man would walk across my range, headin' for the high country."

White Magpie inclined her head slightly. "Sam?"

"I couldn't tell. He was some distance off with his back to me when he came through. Later, I rode after him. Readin' his sign was easy until he cut up into the timber. I lost his tracks, but the sorrel horse kept goin'. I've owned many horses but never one that could follow a blind trail."

"You found Sam in the meadow."

168

Cameron nodded his head. "I seen him a few times in Boulder, one of them old gaffers who live in shacks on the far end of town. We talked a little, then I come back." Cameron felt for his pipe, got it fired up, and wagged his head. "He's old. Been a buffalo hunter. They're all gone now. He was lookin' for a place to make a camp. Sort of set down an' wait."

"Bird come again?" the old woman asked.

Cameron shook his head. "I'm old, too. Old buffalo hunters have nothin'. Nice long-gun with a bird's eye maple stock, not much more. Old man with a good rifle, no family, no money. Been passed by, I expect. I went back. He was . . . well . . . we talked pretty much the same language. I never told him I own that meadow an' around it plumb to the mountains. What difference would it make? There's no country up here I'd dare put cattle on. Feed's not enough, even if there wasn't cow-killin' varmints."

For a long time the old cowman listened to the creek before speaking again. "There's nobody still around who remembers, but, when I was young an' startin' out, I had a Crow woman. She died havin' a child. It died, too."

Cameron sucked at a pipe that had gone out, knocked it empty on his palm, and stole a sidelong look at White Magpie. "Many-Horses come. That old buffalo come. You'n Belle come." He cleared his throat, would not look at her, and set his formidable jaw like a vise for a long time before speaking again. "It pleasured me to bring things up here and see what Sam was doin'. He's got to be as old as I am, but he's tougher'n a boiled owl. The girl's as pretty as her name." He leaned on one elbow in the grass, still avoiding facing her. "You know why I keep comin'?"

She put a hand over her mouth to hide the smile. "White bird make you come."

He swung his head sharply, bushy brows low over steel-blue eyes. "Not the damned bird. I found me a family . . . like folks had when I was young. Even that wore-out old buffalo. When I was young, a man couldn't begin to count 'em. Now they seem all to be gone . . . except for that old cow. Old woman, I kept comin' because it was like things were fifty years back. One high-country meadow an' there it was, a little at a time. Even you'n the girl . . . what's her real name?"

"Yellow Bluebell."

"Yes . . . when you'n Yellow Bluebell come."

The old woman looked away and listened to the creek without speaking for a long time, but eventually she asked: "You know about the Indian circle?"

"I do. My Crow woman taught me." His eyes went to her profile. "Everything is good as long as the circle don't get broke."

She said: "Many-Horses," still looking toward the creek. He, too, looked toward the creek as she spoke again. "The circle. Sam come from the south. Many-Horses come from the east. Yellow Bluebell an' me come from the north. Old buffalo come from the west. That make the circle."

The old cowman lay back in the grass.

White Magpie spoke again. "Yellow dirt . . . ?"

Cameron nodded, without speaking for a while. Then he said: "I knew. Never told no one. I figured maybe Sam, bein' a hunter, wouldn't know ... wouldn't find it."

The old woman wasn't thinking about the gold when she said: "Many-Horses. I miss him."

Cameron agreed. "Good man. I knew his hands an' back hurt him. I figured to bring him down where he could set by the fire. I waited too long."

The old woman raised her eyes. "White bird told me when big moon rise red. Bad comes."

He pushed up into a sitting position with both arms around his knees. "We'll get the buffaloes down with my cattle. You'n Sam come, too, if you want."

"We got plenty wood," she told him."

"Yellow Bluebell . . . ?"

She didn't answer. She went to the creek and drank, washed her face and hands, then stood, looking back at him. "I don't want her to forget the old ways."

He got to his feet, and, while brushing off, he said: "She ain't a child any more. White Magpie, I'd never let her forget the old ways."

"You want to take her?"

"Don't she need better'n what she's had?" He paused. "But you got to come, too."

The old woman knelt again at the creek and splashed water in her face. When she arose, she did not look at him. She started walking back. He did not follow right away. But eventually he did.

Day was ending. The sun would linger, but beyond it there would be another full moon, tinged with red.

When they passed the old cow, she opened her mouth wide and curled her tongue but neither lowered her head nor made a sound.

Sam was measuring rolled barley into the bucket with Yellow Bluebell standing by. Neither looked up as Cameron and the old woman returned.

White Magpie went to the cooking hole. Sam and the cowman sat out front. Yellow Bluebell went inside to her dark place. Once they heard her laugh. Cameron stuffed his pipe. Sam went after his pipe.

There was a noticeable chill as the day ended. Cameron had used up all the tact he possessed out yonder. Now he looked steadily at Sam, trickling smoke, before he said: "We talked about some things. Yellow Bluebell . . ." The pipe went out, and he relighted it, held it in his hand, looking at it, then said: "These things wasn't made for when a man is talkin'. They're like the Injun pipe. They're sort of a ritual." He tucked the pipe away and resumed what he'd been talking about. "You understand about the circle?"

Sam had felt something but shook his head.

"The old woman'll tell you, when she's ready. The circle an' a full moon that rises red."

Sam said: "I'll fetch the bottle."

Cameron shook his head. "Not yet. The circle is completed when things come from four directions. Don't make sense to you, does it?"

"No."

"She'll tell you . . . some day. When Many-Horses died, it broke the circle, an' a big red moon risin' is the sign of bad trouble." Cameron paused, eyeing Sam.

Before continuing, he marshaled words for what he had to say, and used them bluntly. "We'll get the buffaloes down to grass country. The girl . . ."

"Take her down, too," Sam said.

The cowman nodded. "She can't go on livin', always scairt an' hidin'."

"White Magpie?"

"If she wants, fine, but it's hard to say with them old ones."

Sam eased back on the porch. "When I come up here, it was to find a place to maybe hunt'n trap a little. It got pretty complicated after a while."

"Stay up here, if you want," Cameron said. "Come down yonder if you want."

Sam settled back, regarding Andrew Cameron. "I cut feed for stockmen years back. Otherwise, I don't know much about your way of livin'."

Cameron shrugged thick shoulders. "You won't have to work. I hire riders for that, Sam. As long as Carville an' Billy Grover know there's gold up here, they'll haunt you. Some mornin' you'll wake up to a gunshot an' a slug through your head, if you're lucky. Otherwise, they'll shove your feet in a fire."

"I got no cache, Mister Cameron."

The old man's steely eyes showed a gallows' smile. "They'll never believe you. Sam, somethin' told you to start walkin', an' you come up here. A bird?"

"Bird? No, I just had to get away from folks and stores. I started walkin', that's all. I saw the high country and started walkin'."

Cameron's gaze was unwavering. "Maybe the old woman'll stay, too. I don't know. She's old. She's always lived her way. But the girl is young an' deserves better."

Cameron got to his feet, grimaced, and heaved most of his weight to his good leg. When he was able to ease weight on the troublesome leg, he said: "I'll go home. You mind your back."

The two women, and the thin tall old man standing with them, watched until Cameron on his big sorrel horse had passed from sight. White Magpie said: "They'll ambush him."

Sam shrugged — maybe, but he doubted it. The cowman had demonstrated something. He could draw fast and shoot straight, even in the dark.

The women went inside where candlelight made grotesque shadows, but Sam remained outside, smoking his pipe. The old cowman was right. A pipe stayed lighted when the smoker didn't talk.

In the morning Sam Sloan sent Yellow Bluebell out to the buffalo with her bucket and watched the calf cast aside all its wild animal inhibitions and run to meet her. The old cow watched for a long time, but the scent was strong, and eventually she came, too. This time Yellow Bluebell spilled grain on the ground, got the rope around the calf's neck, and, after a few tugs, it followed — not the girl but the smell of the grain in the bucket she carried.

White Magpie came out also to watch, then went around to her cooking hole. She was quiet, more so than usual, which Sam noticed and correctly guessed the reason. The old woman and the old cowman had been out by the creek a long time the day before. In fact, they hadn't come back until sundown.

He went around to hunker near her, continuing to watch Yellow Bluebell and the buffalo. She had her lined old face pinched against rising smoke and acted as though he was not there. They neither faced each other nor looked at one another. Sam was waiting. She eventually said: "Yellow Bluebell can't be Indian forever."

Sam nodded, without taking his eyes off the girl leading the buffalo calf. "No. I come up here to find a place to maybe make a cabin, hunt a little, an' never go back."

"You find place," she said dryly. "You find place because bird guide you, the same as me'n Yellow Bluebell done, like *tatanka* an' Many-Horses done. We all walked to this place."

Sam finally turned. Yellow Bluebell was returning. Her session with the calf was completed for this day. He looked at the old woman. "It's a big meadow. Ain't many ones like it in the mountains."

The old woman batted smoke away. Through it she looked at him. Her face was contorted. Her eyes were wet. She looked a hundred years old, as wrinkled as a prune, with black eyes as shrewd and knowing as the eyes of an old cougar. "Change now."

He nodded. "I expect so."

"Yellow dirt *dina sica*. No good."

He lowered his head as he nodded.

"Circle broke," she muttered, and that brought his head up.

"What in hell is this circle? Mister Cameron talked about it."

She moved away from the smoke, her movements monkey-like. She picked up a scantling of fat wood as she said: "You look."

He watched her draw a circle in the dust. When it was completed, she poked an indentation above the circle, below it, and at both outer sides. She looked up, saw that he was faintly scowling but watching, and poked the stick in the lower hole. "South. You walk from south." She poked another indentation. "Many-Horses come from east." She poked the next indentation. "*Tatanka* come from west." As she touched the last indentation, she said: "Old woman an' girl come from north." She dropped the stick. "That made circle. That make circle whole. You see?"

"I see, we all come together from four directions."

She put a claw-like hand to cover her mouth as she smiled at him. "Now, you watch," she told him and erased the four indentations and in their place made squiggles, each different. She touched the northernmost squiggle. "From here comes water." She touched another squiggle. "From east come sun . . . fire." At the next mark she said: "Air," and moved to the final squiggle as she patted the earth where she was squatting. "Ground."

He nodded again, still faintly frowning.

"Four places . . . north, south, east, west . . . comes the places that make life." She looked up when Yellow

176

Bluebell appeared, smoothed out the circle she had made, and told the girl to go feed her mouse. When she was gone, the old woman looked at Sam. "Circle don't be broke, life is good. Circle is broke, no good."

He raised a puzzled gaze, and she spoke again, looking steadily at him. "Bird make us all walk to this place. It was good."

Sam nodded. A little trying at times, but good. He said: "Yes."

"White Bird only can make good things come."

A flicker of understanding shone in Sam's eyes. "An' the circle got broke when Many-Horses died."

"No! Circle got broke when you bring yellow dirt. Many-Horses knew. There was a sign in the sky, too. I told him. He died when that sign came."

Sam had to stand up. He considered the old woman. "Mister Cameron knows this?"

"Yes."

"How? He don't like Injuns."

White Magpie also arose. "Ask him, not me," she said, and headed for the cabin.

Sam returned to the bench and fired up his pipe. A man doesn't live into his late sixties — maybe seventies — not knowing there is more that he can't find answers to than things he can. Sam had been around Indians all his adult life, never as friends nor even hunting companions. In Sam's frontier world Indians were *there*, and that was all there was to it.

He and White Magpie did not speak to each other for the balance of the day. They both listened to Yellow Bluebell's enthusiastic account of her progress leading the buffalo calf. If she noticed more than usual silence between them, she did not heed it. For one thing, her mouse had brought another mouse to live in the nest with her, but it was very wild. Just a shadow sent it flying to the hole in the roof where it disappeared.

CHAPTER
FOURTEEN

The Low Country

Four days later, with the sun dazzling bright, the days warm but losing warmth quickly after sunset, the meadow grass whose lower parts had turned from tan to brown was now drooping slightly from the weight of seed heads. Sam saw wraiths among trees along the ridge of the east slope. He watched briefly, got his rifle, and went into the shadows by the kindling stack on the same side of the house.

White Magpie appeared in the doorway, also looking up the slope but not for long. She went around to her cooking hole on the west side and carefully fed fat wood slivers into the ash to encourage smoke first, then a finger of fire.

The horsemen emerged at the place where Andrew Cameron had been making his stop for months. Sam leaned the rifle aside. He had no difficulty recognizing the big sorrel horse and the thick shape in the saddle, but the second rider held his attention the longest. It was a younger man, clearly a stockman from the way he sat his saddle.

The cowman began the descent with the younger rider behind him. He twisted once to speak to the younger horseman. All Sam could hear was something which ended in: "Old buffalo."

Sam returned to the doorway, discreetly leaned his rifle inside, and was ready when the riders approached. He called a greeting, and the old stockman replied.

Later, as Cameron was dismounting, he squinted in the direction of the buffalo calf. He said: "Is it broke to lead yet?"

Sam said that it was, that Yellow Bluebell had been teaching it for many days, and he smiled. "I ain't sure which it follows, Yellow Bluebell or the bucket."

The old man gimped his leg briefly, then jerked his head in the direction of the younger rider. "This here is Luc Pernell. I brought him along because I think now's the time to take the old girl an' her calf to the low country."

Before Sam could speak, the old woman appeared in the doorway. She acknowledged Cameron's introduction to the stranger without taking her eyes off Cameron. "You eat?" she asked.

Cameron nodded. "Hour ago." He handed the young rider one rein, looped the other rein around the saddle horn, and jerked his head. He and White Magpie went around to the cooking hole where the cowman said: "You'n the girl ready?"

She considered a thin tendril of smoke arising from the cooking hole. Cameron addressed her again, this time with the gruffness absent. "It's for the best." When she remained silent, he also said: "She's like your own. I know. When a body lives as long as you'n me have lived, we brace against the hurt of loneliness. You come

180

with us, too. Today we'll take the buffaloes down to warm country."

She went as far as the corner of the cabin. He watched her for a moment, then passed around to the broken stone circle, and with one booted foot shoved encircled stones to make another break. He looked at her. She would not meet his gaze. He made a slight gesture of hopelessness and went over to where Sam and the A C Connected rider were standing in awkward silence. He asked if Sam could get a shank on the calf, and Sam shook his head. "Not likely. Only Yellow Bluebell's been workin' at it."

Cameron's exasperation showed when he said: "One way or another it's got to be done. Luc'n I didn't make the long ride up just to go back with nothin'."

The old woman came around front and softly called through the doorway. She had to repeat the call and say something in Crow before Yellow Bluebell came timidly to the doorway. She darted one look at the grizzled old cowman with the bushy brows and bear-trap mouth, then did the same with the stranger, except for an almost imperceptible widening of the eyes, then she looked at the ground until the old woman said in English: "Go get calf. They come to take 'em down out of here."

Tears welled. Yellow Bluebell looked again at Andrew Cameron and, for her, showed surprising defiance when she said: "No! No one take 'em!"

The others were silent for a few moments before the old woman spoke again, this time in Crow, after which Yellow Bluebell turned her back, got the rope from

181

inside, and, with her face averted, took the bucket, and started toward the creek.

Cameron sank down on the bench. When the old woman came to stand beside him, he quietly said: "This ain't goin' to be easy."

"She knows," the old woman told him. "I talk every day to her. She cries. We all cry when things change."

"You ride with her," the old cowman said, watching Yellow Bluebell in the middle distance, and swung his head when the old woman said: "No."

Cameron seemed about to arise from the bench. "No? You got to! She'll be scairt leavin' what she knows up here, ridin' back with just us men."

White Magpie was also watching the girl. The calf was giving trouble, not about the rope but because it wanted to play. It ran around Yellow Bluebell, wrapping her in the rope, until she abruptly sat down in the grass with both hands over her face. Then the calf came up and nuzzled her.

White Magpie made a small sound of personal anguish before she spoke again. "I come with you," she told Cameron, and went inside the cabin to make two traveling bundles, one larger than the other. Her eyes were moist. Her nearly toothless mouth was deliberately held tightly closed. She paused once to look up through the hole in the roof before shaking her head and returning to the bundles.

Yellow Bluebell returned with the calf following on a slack lead. Its mother was slow to understand, but, when she started after her calf, she roared and lumbered with her mouth wide, the pink tongue curled.

182

Luc started forward, sure the cow would trample the girl. White Magpie spoke sharply to him from the doorway: — "No! Stay away!"

Luc would have ignored the command, but Cameron growled: "Leave it be, boy." Anyone who had worked for Andrew Cameron knew that tone of voice. Luc stopped.

The cow reached her calf, lowed, and tried to nudge it away. The calf, like most calves, had a full belly and was not to be turned back. It dodged its mother's head. Yellow Bluebell looked back only once. When she was close, the old man told his rider to mount up and sit still.

The cow rammed to a stiff-legged halt, little eyes dangerously bright. She dropped her head, bellowed, and pawed dirt.

The calf, with its head in the bucket, ignored her, but the two-legged creatures didn't. Sam spoke quietly. If there was one thing he understood, it was buffalo. They were more unpredictable than the weather.

"Just set still. If she charges, run for it. Give her slack'n she may not fight." He addressed Yellow Bluebell in the same quiet tone. "Start up the slope. Don't let the calf have no more grain until you reach the ridge."

Yellow Bluebell did not look at the cowman. She looked directly at Sam. "No hurt cow."

Sam nodded. "She'll foller. We'll foller behind. Don't act scairt an' don't move fast." He tipped his head toward the slope.

As Yellow Bluebell started walking with the calf following like a dog, Sam, the mounted man, and White Magpie watched the old cow. She did as she'd done other times. She waited until her calf was half way up the slope, then she didn't bellow. She made a mother's lowing sound, ignored the motionless two-legged things, and went trotting up the slope. Luc, who knew nothing about buffalo, said: "This might be easier'n we figured, Mister Cameron."

The old man put an expressionless gaze on the younger man and spoke gruffly: "Tell me that when we're out of the timber."

Sam and White Magpie followed the horsemen. Sam carried his rifle loosely. Both he and the old woman were accustomed to traveling distances on foot. Where it was possible, she walked at his side. When forest giants made that impossible, she walked behind him, her mouth still in that bear-trap position.

The old cow did not lessen her defiance, but, when she balked, pawed, and bellowed, Yellow Bluebell let the calf put its head into the bucket. The old cow had to relent, at least to the extent of making little impromptu rushes to travel with her baby some distance, before taking another of her defiant moments of pawing and bellowing.

Sam told the old woman things were progressing better than he had thought they would. She said nothing. Her sinewy old wrinkled legs were like rawhide. She never faltered. Sam eyed her askance once. She had to be older than dirt.

Sam thought they might stop to rest. The old cow was soaked with sweat and obviously both tired and thirsty. Cameron did not even pause. He wanted to be in open country before dusk arrived. They had covered roughly half the distance when he spoke to the rider. "When we get to where we can see out, ride ahead an' make sure there ain't no bulls. I don't think the old girl'll be bullin', but she'll settle in quicker if there ain't bulls to snort her up."

The younger man nodded, then said: "She'll scare hell out of the cows."

Cameron did not reply. He was seeking a break in the timber. It never took much to stampede cattle who were at least half Texas longhorn, and, if they ran, they would run out of fear and breath long before they got anywhere near a terminus of his range.

The buffalo cow did not stop showing defiance, particularly if those bringing up the rear got closer than she liked, but Sam was right: she was tiring. Even her periods of pawing and bellowing challenges were interspersed with lengthy periods when she simply plodded along either beside or directly behind her calf.

The downhill grade seemed to be lessening when Yellow Bluebell called back to White Magpie in Crow that the bucket was almost empty.

The old woman called back in the same language. "Don't let it have so much."

Sam guessed about this exchange and, while watching the girl up ahead, spoke as much to himself as to the old woman. "I don't know nothin' about 'em but, since she's been on the trail, seems to me she don't think about being scairt."

White Magpie shot a glance at the lean old buffalo hunter and did not say a word.

Luc Pernell suddenly rode ahead in a kidney-damaging trot. The old man twisted to call back: "Another couple of miles." He looked down at Yellow Bluebell and made an attempt to do something he'd never been able to do very well — compliment someone. He said: "You done yourself right proud, young lady."

She looked straight ahead. Her hand holding the lead shank was sweaty. She was getting tired and wanted something almost more than the end of this trip — a drink of cold water.

A slight annoying thought came to bother Sam. He called ahead to ask Cameron if he thought cattle might frighten the old cow enough so she'd head back to the meadow.

The old man's answer was brusque. "We'll wait an' see."

Luc returned on a hard-breathing horse. He had found no bulls out on the grassland, but he'd found a fairly large bunch of cows with calves. Cameron nodded. The most docile cow on earth can become a dangerous juggernaut if she perceives even a slight peril to her calf, and all the A C Connected cows had large infusions of longhorn blood. Longhorn were notorious for attacking even mounted men, which the bred-up and shorter-legged range cattle would not do. Someone on foot, yes, someone on horseback, no.

Luc eased back to tell Yellow Bluebell it would only be a short distance now, and, when she looked straight ahead, he smiled. "There's a creek," he told her, and went up to again ride stirrup with Cameron to whom he said: "That's a long hike."

The grizzled old man replied that it had all been downhill, which ended the conversation.

Sam could see open country where the timber had been thinned out for firewood and building material. He spoke aside to the old woman. "They'll have ransacked hell out of the cabin by now."

She did not reply nor even look up. She smiled behind her hand and said nothing, but she doubted the cabin would be ransacked.

When they broke clear of timber, the sun bore down. Cameron led them to a creek and sat his saddle, watching them all tank up, even the agitated old buffalo cow. While waiting, he ranged a wide gaze around, saw only distant bunches of grazing cattle, and told the others they would take the buffalo a mile or so on southward. He wanted to put more ground under the old cow's feet to discourage any back-tracking notion she might get.

For the first time the calf pushed past Yellow Bluebell to crop grass. The old cow came to nuzzle, but the calf ignored her, which was when the old man said: "A sight longer an' they can go free."

He looked down at Yellow Bluebell. She returned his glance but swiftly and uncomfortably.

The sun was lowering. There would still be at least five or six hours of daylight. By the time the old man told Yellow Bluebell to take the rope off, the cow was willing to slog along, tired and a little foot-sore. They expected the calf to make one of its tail-over-the-back runs, but it did not stop grazing as it walked. The old cow did the same. She only discovered her calf was free when it threw up its head, looking for her, and rushed to the right side to suck, its tail wiggling with each swallow. Where they finally halted, Sam saw rooftops in the distance where huge old unkempt cottonwood trees grew. He looked at the old man who looked back and nodded. It was the A C Connected home place.

A light breeze ruffled grass and sifted through the manes of the horses. This was the moment Andrew Cameron had doubts about. He said: "We'll get an early start in the mornin' an' go back to the meadow. Sam, me, an' Luc." He gravely considered the old woman. "You know about cook stoves. There's a storehouse full of tinned things. There's firewood on the east porch." He paused because White Magpie was looking unblinkingly at him from an expressionless face. He started over. "We got to go back. If we don't, no one'll ever be able to sleep up there without a gun in his hand."

The old woman switched her black gaze to Yellow Bluebell and very slowly and very reluctantly nodded her head. After Cameron had ridden on, she watched his back and almost smiled.

When they reached the yard, Luc took the horses to be cared for, and Yellow Bluebell went as far as the wide, doorless opening of the barn to watch. If he knew she was there, he gave no indication of it.

188

White Magpie came soundlessly beside the girl, touched her, and jerked her head. The other two men were on the porch. White Magpie walked behind Yellow Bluebell. She was old. She knew things. It usually happened in springtime when sap ran and wild flowers grew, but she also knew it could happen any time.

Cameron took them inside. His house was large and gloomy. There were layers of dust. In the kitchen unwashed plates were on a round table. The kindling box was full. There were heavy iron pans and kettles. The place smelled of horse and human sweat as well as ingrained pipe smoke from years back.

He told Sam to sit, and they'd have coffee. He took the old woman to the kitchen and left her to fire up the stove.

When the old man returned to the parlor and sank down into a leather chair, he said: "We'll end it tomorrow, Mister Sloan. One way or another we'll end it." He paused to grope for his pipe. As he was stuffing it, he said: "I got to hire a couple of riders. Me'n Luc can't do it all, just the pair of us." He got the pipe fired up. "I'll make sure no one goes up there. I own the land for a couple miles farther up. As far as the base of the mountains. I'll make sure you ain't bothered."

Sam regarded the old man steadily. "You own the meadow?"

"An' a sight farther," Cameron replied, tamping the pipe with a callused thumb.

White Magpie brought coffee, hot enough to scald a brass cat. They put the cups aside, and White Magpie retreated beyond the open kitchen door and listened as the cowman said: "The girl . . . what's her name?"

"Yellow Bluebell. It's easier to just say Belle."

Cameron nodded. "Me'n the old woman talked. The girl deserves better'n a life of hidin' an' bein' scairt."

Sam tested the coffee which was still too hot and put it aside again. What the cowman was saying had little to do with Sam. He asked if White Magpie approved, and Cameron removed the pipe before answering. "Mister Sloan, with Injuns you can't be sure what they think. I reasoned with the old woman. I'm right. The girl's comin' along toward being grown. In another five or ten years she'll know everything she grew up with ain't no more. I'll make sure she don't forget the old ways, but . . . I never had a family. Once I almost had." Cameron paused to relight the pipe. "I want to see she gets the best. She's got to grow up understandin' our world, yours an' mine. She'll have more'n one dress, a horse of her own, maybe even some folks her age over in Boulder. I know, she's an Injun. She'll run into that all her life, but hidin' in the mountains, livin' off bear meat and roots . . ." The old man waited until he had another full head of smoke rising before continuing. "I want her to grow up understandin' how the world works. If she keeps on bein' Injun, she'll likely die young, scairt all the time." Cameron gave up on the pipe, knocked it empty into a plate, and put it on the table where the plate was. As he settled back in the chair, he said: "Old woman, come here."

White Magpie appeared in the kitchen doorway but came no farther. Cameron gazed at her. "You heard. I saw your shadow behind the door. Only thing I didn't say was you got to stay here with her. It'll make the change easier. You won't have to do nothin' but help her adjust. White Magpie, I can't do it without you. You know what she's goin' up against. Without you I can't do it, an' she deserves better'n she's had."

White Magpie regarded the lined, weathered old face with its direct steely eyes, and nodded. She then went back where the stove needed filling. They heard her noisily lifting the burner plates and putting wood in, then closing the plates.

Andrew Cameron arose, winced until his leg stopped hurting, and took Sam outside. At the door he dryly said: "You won't need the rifle," and waited until Sam had leaned it in a corner.

Dusk was settling as the pair of old men crossed the yard to the barn. It was gloomy inside, but it was also fragrant. There was curing timothy in the loft — horse feed. The cattle foraged.

They went on through to the set of pole corrals. Luc was out there, salving an old mare where she had been bitten. Luc turned, nodded, and went back to doctoring the mare.

Cameron leaned on the stringers. There were six horses in the corrals, using animals, never more than six — that was all the hay he put up each summer for corralled using horses which could not forage.

Sam leaned too, watching the young rangeman and studying the horses. Men learned, particularly men who had depended upon horses during the hunt, to know how hard riding a short-backed horse was, and how fast a tall, narrow horse was, and how lack of care ruined horses, but Sam had never been a rangeman. He told Andrew Cameron the horses looked good, and the old man turned toward him almost smiling. What did buffalo hunters, or men who walked rather than rode, know about horses, but he nodded as he said: "Don't pay to keep horses that ain't good, Mister Sloan." He changed the subject. "We got to start early in the mornin', an' we got to go a different route. Carville an' Billy Grover'll be watchin'." Cameron nodded as Luc left the corral on his way to the barn with the salve pail. "Mister Sloan, I'm goin' to hang those two. Not near the meadow, out through the forest somewhere. Not over the gold but for takin' my horses without permission. It's called horse stealin', an' as far back as I can remember it's been a hangin' offense."

Luc did not come out to join them. On their way back to the house they saw weak candlelight coming from the log bunkhouse. The old man said: "They're hard to find, Mister Sloan, especially young as Luc is. Hard workin', honest as the day is long, takes care of animals, not the best roper I've ever had, but good enough. An' don't poke his nose where it don't belong."

When they reached the porch, White Magpie appeared, holding a bottle and two tin cups. She and the cowman exchanged a long look, then she went back inside.

As they sat, Sam watched the cups being partly filled and said: "Mister Cameron, sure as we're settin' here, there'll be others. Even without Grover an' Carville spillin' the beans, there'll be others. Gold just naturally attracts folks."

The cowman got resettled in a chair, pushed gently to position one leg where he wanted it, sipped, and said: "I expect that's right, but no one ever heard about it from me, an' after we settle with Grover an' Carville ..." The old man sipped again before continuing. "You're likely right," he said, and looked at Sam. "You found it, an' you're a hunter, not a miner. Well, you got my word there won't be nobody go up there. I'll give them orders to the new men I got to hire."

For a while they sipped watered whiskey and were quiet. Eventually Sam quietly said: "You can't tell 'em to keep out of the mountains. Grover an' Carville got curious."

Cameron drained his cup and stood up. "We ought to set out early," he said, and pointed. "There's plenty of room at the bunkhouse. Good night."

As the old man bedded down, he thought Sam was right. He hadn't told Grover and Carville not to follow him, to stay clear of the mountains. He sighed. Sometimes in life futility was epitomized by peeing in a river, expecting it to rise. People did just about as they pleased. If they were curious, they sure as hell did.

He dropped off, thinking of the old woman and the girl. He'd be gone all day and maybe more. If they were gone when he got back . . . ? He slept.

CHAPTER
FIFTEEN

The Unexpected

When they left the yard the following morning, the old woman watched from a parlor window. Later she roused Yellow Bluebell who was a sound sleeper any time, but, in a large room where she had made a small lump in a big bed, it was like awakening the dead. Presently they explored the house, the yard, the barn, and the sheds. They hauled four buckets of water to the kitchen. The tank on the side of the stove held three gallons.

White Magpie did something which was out of character for her. She talked of many things, not even slacking off until the sun was high, the same sun that was piercing treetop canopies infrequently as the old cowman allowed his large sorrel horse to pick its way through thick stands of mighty fir giants.

He was familiar with the path he was taking, but it had been years since he had ridden it. His jaw was set. His steely eyes beneath shaggy eyebrows missed nothing. The only time he halted was when they could see the cabin from among timber from the west side. For a while no one spoke. Out across the meadow, which was empty now, the house seemed deserted and forlorn. A coyote sounded.

The old man resumed the ride northward. Sam had an idea what he was doing but kept it to himself. Luc Pernell simply followed, expressionless and silent. When the old man angled easterly, they eventually reached the log landing. There he stopped again. This time he sat with both hands atop the saddle horn, a massive silhouette in his sheep-pelt coat. Eventually he said: "Well, Mister Sloan?"

Sam's reply was cryptic. "Up the creek. Foller it to where there's a little waterfall."

The old man reined north up the skid trail. Luc had a question for Sam. "You don't figure they'd be at the house?"

Sam didn't answer. The old man did.

"There'd have been horses out grazin' if they was."

When the old man said this, his gaze met Sam's and slid away. If Luc didn't know about the gold . . . ?

Cameron growled and pointed earthward. There was one set of boot tracks where the ground was soft, deep tracks made by someone whose hike showed signs of an erratic stride. The old man grunted. "Whiskey for breakfast. We'll find him."

It did not happen exactly that way. Billy Grover found them. They hadn't made a lot of noise, and, if it had only been one rider or someone on foot, there wouldn't have been any noise, but in the deathless silence three mounted men made noise, not much but enough.

The old man was erect in the saddle with the tie-down hanging loosely over his holstered Colt. Sam, who was directly behind the big sorrel, freed up his belt gun, and Luc did the same.

The burly bearded rangeman surprised them, more by his physical appearance than by coming suddenly from behind a tree. His trousers were wet to the knees. He was hatless, and instead of a belt gun he was holding a Winchester saddle gun. He yelled at the old man: "You old son of a bitch!"

The old man rested both hands atop the horn and did not raise his voice when he said: "Good afternoon, Billy. Where's your horse?"

Sam and Luc were poised, scarcely breathing. The burly rangeman's eyes were wild as they moved from one mounted man to the others.

The old man spoke again, quietly. The echo was as resonant as the voice that had made it. Cameron said: "Where's Jed?"

Grover wigwagged with the Winchester. "Get down, you old bastard. Tried to keep it secret . . . about the gold, didn't you? But I didn't come down in the last rain. *Get down!*"

Cameron did not move. His sunk-set steely gaze was fixed on the bearded man. "Put the gun down, Billy."

"I'll kill you, you cranky, mean old . . ."

The explosion was so loud and unexpected the horses reacted violently. Under the hands of men to whom these reactions to gunfire were nothing new they were held to a minimum of lunging.

196

Billy Grover bled like a stuck hog until the man who had shot him dismounted, grimaced, leaned on the saddle a moment, then went where the burly man was no longer breathing.

Luc said: "You beat me to it, Mister Cameron. He was crazy . . . didn't even have the carbine cocked."

The old man nodded, returned to his horse, and mounted. "Jed'll have heard the shot," he said, and reined eastward, leaving his companions to follow or not.

Sam knew every inch of this area. They would top out above the cabin on the slope where the view was excellent. On the east side was where White Magpie hoarded fat wood and bundles of dry grass.

They hesitated some distance northward. They could see the house through trees. Sam took the lead. He knew better places to make a sighting.

Where they finally stopped and tied the horses to low limbs, Sam led the way to the last tier of trees. From there they could count knotholes in the log walls.

In front, near the sticky seated chairs and the bench, two men had flung horse gear indiscriminately. The old man commented on that. "They had just one thing in mind. The cache."

The old man's observation may have meant nothing to Luc, but Sam almost imperceptibly nodded as he said: "Where is the son of a bitch?"

They hunkered in long silence. Luc was concerned only with whom they were seeking. That's all he wanted to know. He was not a man given to asking questions.

Cameron fished out his little pipe and sucked on it. Sam carefully scrutinized the area. Eventually his gaze returned to the cabin. "Something's wrong," he murmured, and Cameron inclined his head without speaking until he'd pocketed the little pipe, then he spoke. "If he'd been up yonder with Grover, we'd have routed him out when we come around to this place. Maybe the scrawny little bastard found the cache, let Billy go up yonder, an' run for it."

Sam looked at the old man. He knew there was no cache. Sam had told him so. Sam said nothing and returned to studying the cabin. He finally arose to lead off very cautiously down the slope to the side of the house where the kindling had been stacked.

The only audible sound as they pressed ears against the log wall was the sound of tiny feet running along the ridge in the direction of the hole in the roof. Sam said nothing. If it had been Belle's mouse, she probably would have come to the edge to peer downward.

Sam whispered to Luc to go around to the west side and wait for Sam's signal. He and the cowman would make a run at the door. As the younger man moved off, Sam whispered: "I got a feelin' this ain't the first time . . . for me anyway."

Cameron wasn't interested in talk. He lifted out his sidearm and waited for Sam to give the signal after knowing Luc was in place. The plain fact was that Andrew Cameron's hearing had been deteriorating for several years.

Sam leaned to peer around. There was not a sound inside the house. Luc eased his head around. He and

Sam exchanged a look before Sam pulled back to tell Cameron to be careful when he fired. Sam would be in front of him, he reminded the old cowman, and got back a look that would have withered a stone.

Sam took down a breath and sprang around the corner with Cameron behind but a yard or two on Sam's left. Luc came around, too.

They saw Jed Carville. He had a holstered Colt. His hat was half beneath the table. He was flat down and unmoving, but he had moved. There were long scratch marks on the floor which led to his curled fingers.

The old man shouldered his companions aside, stood over Carville, gun cocked and ready, then eased off the dog, holstered his six-gun, and sank to one knee to roll Carville onto his back. "Deader'n hell," he intoned, sounding, and looking, baffled.

Sam and Luc came near to join Cameron, staring at the dead man. Cameron groped for a wound of some kind and found none. He lifted his hat briefly to scratch vigorously, stood up, and looked at Sam and his rider as though they could provide an answer.

They couldn't.

The cabin had been ransacked again, more thoroughly this time because Grover and Carville had watched the odd procession the day before when the old cow and her calf had been taken down out of the high country. It required no particular astuteness to see that the dead man had eaten and had used all the candles after nightfall to make an inch-by-inch search.

Cameron sent Luc to fetch the horses while he and Sam did some rummaging on their own. Four of the candles had burned down to puddles of wax before dying. Some of White Magpie's hoard under Sam's bunk had been taken to the table and cut into slabs. The whiskey bottle, which had been about half full, was on the table, stopper lying in cold wax. Sam eyed it until the old man reached to hoist it, stopped his hand in mid-lift, wrinkled his nose, and put the bottle down. He told Sam not to touch it and scuffed among débris until he found the blue bottle. It was empty. He put it in a pocket as Luc appeared in the doorway.

They went outside. The sun was high. Visibility was perfect, and, although the day was warm, there was also a hint of chill. They used up the balance of the light to bury Grover and Carville. It would have taken half the time if there'd been more than one shovel.

When they had mounded the graves, Sam mentioned a dram of whiskey, and the cowman growled, went inside for the bottle, returned, and up-ended it over the pair of fresh graves with Sam watching, wearing a puzzled expression. It was a little shy of sundown.

From the topout along the easterly rim Sam stopped to look back. Cameron did the same. Before he and Sam turned away, the cowman cast a sidelong look at the old buffalo hunter. Instinct told him what he suspected. Sam Sloan would never return to this meadow.

They rode for hours, until dusk had come and gone, without any of them saying a word. About the time they should have been able to see open country, the old cowman fired up his little pipe. Tonight the moon would not arise for several hours, and, when it came, it wouldn't be much more than a curved sliver.

They reached grassland. Near the creek the cowman had to halt, get down, and, while leaning on his horse, stood like a stork, one leg off the ground. With his face inches from the saddle's loop-through, he gruffly said: "You fellers go on. I'll be along."

Sam and Luc had also dismounted. Neither moved.

Sam said: "It ain't none of my business, but you'd ought to see a doctor."

Cameron answered characteristically, still leaning. "You're right. It ain't none of your business. There's no medicine man closer'n Durango up in Colorado."

He moved to hoist his leg to the stirrup, got the boot settled, but, when he started to heave himself into the saddle, the leg gave way. The old man sprawled as his sorrel horse moved clear and looked around.

Humiliated beyond endurance, the old man sat on the ground and cursed for two minutes without repeating himself. When Luc and Sam moved toward him, Cameron swore at them too, rolled over, got a grip on the left stirrup, and hauled himself upright. This time, when he raised his leg, Luc and Sam boosted him from behind. Cameron grabbed leather with both hands to keep himself from going off on the right side, swore and growled until he was erect, then jerked his head.

They continued in the direction of the home place in absolute silence. The old man felt for his pipe and mightily swore again. He had lost it when he had fallen back yonder. Sam offered his pipe. The old man glowered and shook his head. "I had that pipe since the Crow woman gave it to me."

When they reached the yard, it was not only dark in all directions, it was also cold. Luc led the horses away to be cared for. Sam stayed close beside the old man until they reached the three long, broad steps leading to the porch. Then, when Sam offered an arm, Cameron ignored it and with jaws clamped like a vise climbed each step by using his left hand to raise and lower his left leg.

As he sank down in a chair, Sam said: "I'll get a bottle."

Cameron sat hunched inside his sheep-pelt coat, staring stonily ahead. When Sam returned, the old man held the bottle at arm's length, and, after Sam had pulled on it a couple of times, the old man did, too.

He removed the bottle he'd brought from the cabin, set it on the porch railing, and stared at it. Sam's back hadn't hurt until he and Luc had bent to hoist the cowman into the saddle. From that point on he'd had to grit his teeth. Cameron offered him the bottle, and Sam took two more long pulls, before handing it back.

Cameron said: "You ever hear it said that whiskey'n rare meat ain't good for folks?"

Sam had never heard such a ridiculous statement in all his life, but he nodded.

Cameron's whiskey was working. His leg no longer hurt. He said: "Mister Sloan, it ain't rare meat an' whiskey that's bad for folks. It's old age. I been livin' with the leg an' fightin' everythin' else a long time. Have another pull."

He passed the bottle. Sam drank and passed it back for Cameron to swallow a couple of times. He was sweating inside the sheep-pelt coat, and, although his tiredness lingered, as long as he sat without moving, it did little more than make him drowsy. Usually after a long day the weariness brought aches. Not this time.

He said: "The old woman bedded down, is she?"

Sam fuzzily thought he'd ought to know whether she was or not, so, when he replied, he sounded a little guilty. "I expect she is. You want her? I'll . . ."

"No, let her sleep. Mister Sloan, did you ever know an Injun like her?"

"No, can't say that I have."

"You know what killed Jed Carville?"

"No, but I'm satisfied he'n Grover are dead."

The old man's head dropped. Within moments he was snoring. For a while Sam remained on the porch. Increasing chill finally drove him to the bunkhouse where Luc was making noises like a shoat caught under a fence.

In the morning Sam was alone in the bunkhouse. He got dressed and went out back to the washstand. If he'd been at the cabin, he could have shaved.

Sunlight hurt his eyes, so he tipped his hat down in front. Over at the main house White Magpie and Yellow Bluebell were shelling something into a large pan. Sam went over there. Both the women looked up, but only White Magpie continued to look. Out back somewhere Luc was having trouble with a horse. Yellow Bluebell sprang up and ran down the steps. Sam turned in surprise until the old woman said: "Big man in bed."

Sam returned his attention to the old woman. "Is he all right?"

She jutted her chin in the direction of a two-thirds empty bottle on the railing and went back to shelling small pods.

Sam went inside, paused in the parlor until he heard a bear-like groan, then went in that direction. Someone had put a blanket over the only window. Sam went to the bedside, and the cowman sat up, wiping his eyes. "Where's the old woman?"

"On the porch huskin' beans into a pan."

Cameron groaned as he eased down gingerly. "I need whiskey."

Sam went dutifully to the porch, got the nearly empty bottle, and returned to the bedroom with it. Cameron tilted it, swallowed, blew out a flammable breath, and peered at Sam through eyes that swam in moisture.

Sam asked if he wanted to see the old woman. Cameron lay back in silence and closed his eyes as he sucked air like a fish out of water. "Mister Sloan . . . ?"

"What? I'll fetch her."

"Leave her be. Mister Sloan, how do you feel this mornin'?"

"Like I been yanked through a knothole. You?"

"I think we got drunk last night. Nothin' to eat since breakfast. Pull up that chair."

Sam obeyed and sat down.

204

The old cowman used a large blue bandanna to wipe his eyes, but, when he spoke again, he sounded almost normal. "Mister Sloan, I got some trouble."

Sam waited. The room was sparsely furnished, and what was in it was old, even the bedstead with its four upright posts which had carved pears or some kind of fruit at the top of each post.

"I can't get out of this damned bed."

Sam felt alarm but remained silent.

"I tried three times. I can't lie here. I got to go to town'n hire some riders. It'll be fall directly. Time to make a gather an' cut out what I'll trail down to the railroad corrals." Cameron's voice was strong and normal, gruff and resonant. He still occasionally dabbed at his eyes, but, when he pushed himself up this time, he reached around to ram two pillows into his back. He squinted at Sam. "I can't lie here, Mister Sloan."

"What do you want me to do? I don't know anythin' about cattle."

Cameron swung back the covers as he said: "Help me stand up." Sam helped. Immediately after Cameron was able to stand without help, Sam's back shot pains almost up to his shoulders. He sat down until Cameron said: "Help me into my britches." Sam helped and gritted his teeth. He had to bend to hold boots for the cowman, but, when Cameron was dressed, Sam reached for the chair again. Cameron eyed him. "You'n me got somethin' in common."

"What?"

"Old bones, Mister Sloan. Things are givin' out. Mind if I ask how old you are?"

Sam didn't mind, but he had to hesitate before answering, because he was not sure. He said: "Late sixties, maybe seventies . . . somewhere around there."

Cameron did not smile, but he sounded amused when he said: "You're a youngster, Mister Sloan. I'm eighty-four." The cowman considered the open doorway. "I can likely make it, but if you was to be beside me . . ."

They made it to the parlor where they both sat down. White Magpie appeared in the kitchen doorway. "Eat," she said, and both old men looked half sick.

Cameron gingerly shook his head. "Eat later," he told her. "Come in here an' set down."

She obeyed without hesitation and fixed the cowman with her shrewd bright black eyes. Sam thought she was going to laugh, but she didn't.

Someone else did, though. Somewhere behind the barn Yellow Bluebell laughed, and instantly the old woman's expression changed.

CHAPTER
SIXTEEN

Sundown

Cameron eventually broke the silence. He asked White Magpie if there was coffee. She went quickly to the kitchen, filled two cups, returned, and handed each old man a cup. Sam eyed his askance. The last time she'd made coffee it had been hotter than the hubs of hell.

Cameron sipped, ran a large, callused hand over his face where the bristle was long enough so that Sam and the old woman heard the grating sound. Cameron dabbed at his eyes. White Magpie covered her mouth. Sam inhaled coffee fragrance but made no move to lift the cup.

Andrew Cameron fished in his pockets, brought forth a blue bottle, and put it on the table beside his chair. He looked steadily at the old woman without speaking for a long time. Eventually he said: "Did you know what was in the bottle?"

White Magpie shook her head.

"How come you to empty it in the whiskey bottle?"

Sam's eyes widened. He turned to look at the old woman. Like Cameron, she was slow to speak, but eventually she did.

"I smell it. Strong medicine. Sometime I can't walk right. If smell do that to me, what would it do to those men who was out there?"

Cameron ran his hand over beard stubble again as he looked at Sam. He said: "You old witch. The whiskey killed one an' made the other one crazy."

White Magpie sat without expression, regarding the cowman. "Whiskey make 'em crazy anyway. Blue bottle make them crazier when you find 'em."

"You figured that?"

"Yes."

"Why didn't you tell me? It'd have saved a lot of saddle-backing."

The old woman did not answer. It became clear that she was not going to answer. Cameron drifted his wet gaze back to Sam. "Go outside an' bend over as far as you can. Stay like that for a couple of minutes, then straighten up." At the look he was getting from the other old man, he nodded his head. "It don't last long, but for a short spell you won't have no back pain. Try it."

After Sam left the parlor, the old cowman gazed steadily at White Magpie. "I'm goin' to send Luc up to Durango with a letter to a fee lawyer I know up there."

White Magpie said: "Medicine man?"

Cameron made a derisive snort. "Fee lawyer, not a doctor. Listen to me. My Crow woman died, havin' my baby."

"You told me," the old woman said.

This time Cameron reddened. "Shut up an' just listen."

She nodded.

"White Magpie, the baby was a girl."

She started to speak, and he made a slashing motion with one hand. She did not speak.

"I want you to promise me somethin'. You'll stay here with her for a year or so. She needs you a lot more'n she needs me. I need you to promise me you'll look after her. She's gettin' along to bein' a young woman. You understand?"

White Magpie bobbed her head.

"Someday she's got to go to town."

"They no like Injun."

He nodded slightly. "Explain to her, get her ready. She can't stay out here forever. There's many things you can do. Make it as easy as you can. I know how to handle them things, but I won't be around. White Magpie, Yellow Bluebell is the little girl that died on me along with her mother. If she'd lived . . . ? I was younger then. If she'd lived, I could have settled things before she come to face 'em. You understand what I'm sayin'?"

She understood. In fact she had understood before he had said it all. She said: "Drink coffee," and he obediently reached for the cup. "What happens . . . after?" she asked.

The old man put the emptied cup aside. "There'll be a lot of young bucks want to marry her. You got to be real careful."

"Why they want to marry her?"

"That letter Luc'll take to the fee lawyer up in Durango has my will in it. You understand?"

"No."

"A will is what folks make, so's, after they're dead, it says what they wanted done with what they left behind. Yellow Bluebell is my heir . . . my only heir. An heir is who gets what it says in the will." He studied her face, then sighed, and started over. "White man law says whatever I put in my will goes to whoever I say in the will it goes to."

Her bird-bright eyes did not leave his face. "More than horses?"

"Everything, including horses, all the cattle, all the land, this house we're sittin' in. Every damned thing I own."

White Magpie had been sitting on the edge of her chair. Now she gradually eased back. "You live a long time," she said.

Cameron shook his head. "I'm past eighty years. You understand? I've lived twice as long as most folks. I've been givin' out the last few years. I can't make the gather this autumn. Luc's goin' to hire more riders. He's a good man, young but savvy an' honest. You tell him I said to run things, an' tell him to run off fellers who'll sure as hell come out to marry her after I'm gone. If you don't do them things for me . . ."

"Nobody listen to old Injun woman."

His answer was given in two sentences. "Get me some whiskey," and, as she arose, he also said: "Find Luc an' tell him I want to talk to him."

She returned and placed a bottle on the table beside the empty coffee cup and left the house.

210

She did not leave the porch for a long time, not until she saw Luc and Yellow Bluebell coming out of the barn, talking and laughing. Then she went out to them, told Luc what Mr. Cameron had said, and took Yellow Bluebell back toward the barn.

Sam came out of the bunkhouse, saw them enter the barn, and went back inside to clean his rifle and ponder. The high meadow had bad memories, and one grave he'd have to pass every time he entered or left the cabin. Somewhere in those miles-deep mountains there had to be another place. This time with no yellow dirt. So far no one would find it. He'd have to hurry. Autumn was in the air. He'd take tools from the cabin. If he found a hidden valley, he'd have to work ten hours a day to get a shelter built and winter wood cut and stacked.

He saw Luc cross toward the main house, and for a fleeting moment he reflected how being young with no aches was a good way to be.

The old man was waiting when Luc entered. He motioned toward the chair White Magpie had used, and, as the younger man sat, Cameron offered the bottle. Luc shook his head, held his hat between his knees, and thought the old man was maybe having eye trouble because he used a blue bandanna to wipe them now and then.

Cameron asked if Luc had ever been to Durango and got a negative head shake. "Well, I need you to take a letter up there for me."

Luc did not ask why the letter could not be mailed in Boulder, but he wondered.

As though the old man had read his mind, he said: "I want you to hand it personal to the feller with the address on the letter. If he ain't there, wait. He's got to have it handed to him."

Luc nodded. "Mister Cameron, it'll take four or five days. It's gettin' close to gatherin' time."

Cameron nodded. "When you get back see what you can hire in Boulder. Older riders if you can find 'em. We can make up a drive to rail's end before frost." Cameron arose, held onto the chair briefly, then said: "I'll have the letter written. Come back in an hour. Take what you'll need. Leave the horse with the liveryman in town and take the first stage north."

He closed the door after Luc, went to his littered office where a pretty lady carrying a parasol faced his desk from a four-year-old calendar, sat down, and started writing. He scrapped the first two attempts and labored over the third.

When he returned to the parlor, White Magpie and Yellow Bluebell were busy in the kitchen. They were talking in Crow. The old man remembered very little of it. He went out onto the porch and, when Luc came, handed him the sealed letter. Later, he watched Luc ride out of the yard in the direction of Boulder.

Sam came out of the bunkhouse, saw the old man on the porch, and walked over.

Cameron looked up. "I'll get a bottle," he said without making a move to leave the chair. Sam sat down, very straight, shaking his head. "None for me, if

212

it's all the same. I never was much of a drinkin' man, an' after last night I'm even less of a one."

Cameron gazed broodingly across the yard and beyond. "Care for a little advice, Mister Sloan?"

"Wouldn't object at all."

"Go back up yonder, sack up all the gold you can find, come back down here, an' buy a nice house in Boulder where you can set on the porch."

Sam squinted beyond the yard in the direction of timbered high country. "That's good advice," he said. "An' I'm grateful to you for it."

"But you ain't goin' to take it."

Sam hung fire over his reply. "I can't stand towns but just so long."

"I told you, you're welcome to stay here as long as you want. I like the idea of a couple of old men stayin' warm in winter, tryin' to see who can tell the biggest lie."

The cowman was making Sam uncomfortable. His next words were spoken slowly. "I'd like that, Mister Cameron. Trouble is, I never stayed in one place long."

"An' now you're too old to change?"

"Yes."

"Where'll you go?"

"I don't know. Up to the cabin for a few things. I won't stay long." Sam followed that statement up quickly to change the subject. "You expect that old buffler cow'll get caught by one of your bulls?"

Cameron was slow replying. "I don't know. She's old."

"But she's in good shape."

"Yes. Well, if she does, what in hell kind of calf will it be."

Sam said: "A cattlelo. You might just start a new kind of beef animal." He paused. "I'll be leavin' before dawn . . ."

White Magpie appeared in the doorway. "Eat," she said and did not wait to see them arise, which was just as well because neither of them spoke nor moved for a full two minutes. Finally Cameron reached for the railing to steady himself before entering the house.

An unexpected thing happened the following day. Two grizzled, gray, and weathered riders appeared in the yard, asking for Mister Cameron. When the old man came to the porch, one of the men said: "My name's Sid Moreland. This here is Ed Handly. We met a feller in Boulder said you might need a couple of riders."

The old man studied Moreland and Handly over a period of silence, then said: "The bunkhouse is yonder. I pay regular wages. Settle in, boys. We'll talk in the mornin'."

When he turned to go back inside, White Magpie was waiting. "More riders?"

He nodded. "The kind I like. Been around long enough so's I don't have to tell 'em what to do."

"Good men?" she asked.

He rolled his eyes around to her face. "Can't be as bad as what they'll replace. Any of that fried meat left?"

Moreland and Handly turned out to be seasoned and experienced. They harnessed the top buggy so the old man could go out with them. When they'd checked through hundreds of cattle, they all abruptly halted.

Moreland said: "What in the hell?"

Cameron leaned sideways when he said: "It's an old buffalo. That big critter lyin' beside the tree with her is her calf."

Handly frowned. "I thought they was all gone."

"They are," Cameron said. "We found this one with a cougar on her back, killed the cat, patched her up, and brought her down here to . . . well, do like she's doin'. Set in the shade. She's old."

When they got back, White Magpie and Yellow Bluebell emerged from the barn, saw the hard-looking rangemen with the old man, and froze. Cameron gestured for Moreland to dismount and help him out of the wagon. As he did this, he said: "The old one's White Magpie. The young one's Yellow Bluebell. They belong here."

Later, at the bunkhouse, Handly peered out the tiny front window in the direction of the house. "Buffalo an' squaw Injuns."

Moreland spoke from over by the cook stove. "The Hukaby place had tame antelopes. The Rutherfords had a boy born with one foot out of the stirrup. Look-a-here, this cupboard's full of store-bought grub."

Handly's concern about the old cow and the Indians vanished when he crossed to examine the fully stocked cupboard. He said: "I liked the old man. Don't get around good. We'll eat good, Oswald."

"You know better'n to call me Oswald."

"Sid . . . we'll eat good here."

* ★ ★

The old man drove out with the new riders four days in a row, by which time they scarcely more than glanced at the old buffalo, and she paid about as much attention to them. Her big calf was skittish, but, when the cow wouldn't move, it settled down. Then it was skittish only whenever horsemen appeared.

On the fifth day the old man gimped to the bunkhouse porch and sat down, gazing easterly in the direction of Boulder. The new hands rolled smokes and also sat out there.

The old man abruptly said: "You see a man's gatherings in the bunkhouse? That's Luc's place. L-u-c. Don't ask me why he spells it that way. He'll be back in a few days. When I'm not around, Luc'll be head Injun." The old man fished for his pipe from long habit, remembered he had lost it, shoved up to his feet, and said: "You're wonderin' about the Injuns. The girl's sort of an orphan. The old woman's sort of her mother, or grandmother. I'd wait, if I was you, they scare easy. Good night."

Two days later Luc returned. The old man had sent Handly and Moreland to look for sore-footed bulls, but, after Luc cared for his horse, before appearing at the house he stopped briefly at the bunkhouse.

The old man was waiting on the porch and wasted no time. He said: "You handed the fee lawyer the letter?"

Luc nodded, thumbed back his hat, and sank into a chair. He was tired. "Put it in his hand myself."

"Did he say anything?"

216

"Asked who it was from, an', when I told him, he said thanks and left me standin'."

The old man nodded. "He's sort of short."

Luc nodded. He thought that, since the fee lawyer and Mister Cameron had that in common, it was no surprise the old man had cottoned to the lawyer.

White Magpie appeared in the doorway. Peering over her shoulder and smiling was Yellow Bluebell. She asked if Luc was hungry. He was.

The old woman then said: "Eat," and both women disappeared.

Cameron acted as though this intrusion had not occurred. "I hired them two fellers you sent. So far, I'd say they're good men. I told 'em you'd be boss."

Luc eyed the old man in silence.

Cameron had a little more to say. "You run things, boy. I don't think I'll be able to do much."

"How's the leg, Mister Cameron?"

"Well . . . between you'n me . . . it's not just the leg. There's other things." Cameron looked at the younger man. "The old woman'll stay until Yellow Bluebell figures this is her home, where she belongs." The steely eyes hardened a little. "Mind the new riders don't bother her. I don't think they will, but mind it don't happen anyway. Let's go eat."

Luc made a point of not watching the old man make three attempts to stand before he succeeded and steadied himself by gripping the railing. Luc held the door for him.

In the kitchen White-Magpie heaped two platters, set them before the men, and hovered. Luc gazed at tinned peaches and their juice piled atop his steak and reached for the coffee cup.

Yellow Bluebell topped up Luc's coffee cup before it had been half emptied. She asked him in clearly enunciated and separated words how the trip was.

When he looked up to answer, she dropped her gaze to the floor. "Fine trip," he replied. "Grass up north is dyin' down. Ours hasn't had a bad freeze yet."

At the stove White Magpie listened with her black eyes fixed on the old man. He didn't notice.

After the men had eaten, they did not go all the way to the porch, although the old man's habit for years was to sit out there to watch the sun set. They sat in the parlor. The old man had a whiskey bottle on the table beside his chair and offered it to Luc, who declined. Having been fed, Luc was now ready to sleep a full, long night. Stagecoaches might be a fast way to travel but over rutted roads riding in one was like riding a hobbled horse.

When Luc was finally able to leave, he met Yellow Bluebell on the porch with dusk settling. She said: "Fine you are back," and he wanted to smile at her stilted, perfectly enunciated words.

"I'm glad to be back, Belle. You're lookin' good."

She had exhausted all the boldness she had forced herself to use by ambushing him on the porch. She said: "Good night," and fled.

At the bunkhouse Moreland and Handly reintroduced themselves. Luc nodded from the edge of his bunk while kicking out of his boots. "Glad you made it. I'm wore down. We'll talk some more tomorrow," he said, and sank back atop his blankets, hatless but still wearing his shell belt and holster.

The following morning the pair of new riders busied themselves at the barn and corrals until Luc appeared. It was close to nine o'clock. Neither Handly nor Moreland mentioned that, even though such an excellent opportunity to rag someone did not come often. This time they neither knew their man that well nor had they been working for A C Connected much more than a week.

The three of them left the yard with Yellow Bluebell watching them and White Magpie watching her.

The old man went down to the barn. The old woman saw him crossing the yard, waited, then also headed in that direction. Cameron was sitting in shade on an upended horseshoe keg. He didn't see her until she wanted him to, then all he said was: "It's quiet, ain't it?"

She approached, black eyes intent. "You sick?"

The old man rallied. In his lifelong deep, growling voice he said: "No, I ain't sick. I never been sick in my life!"

"Your leg?"

"Well, gawd dammit, a man's got a right to have a sore leg now'n then." His glaring look softened. "Set down, White Magpie."

She sat on the hardpan floor.

He looked around the barn and back to her tilted face. "I run out of breath lately." He paused, pushed up a small smile, and added: "Before you was born, I hauled down the logs an' built this barn."

Her expression did not show that she didn't believe he had done anything before she was born.

"You take good care of Yellow Bluebell," he said.

"I take care. You see how she looks an' acts around Luc?"

He had noticed nothing. "Well, he's a good man. Hard to come across honest folks any more."

"She likes him."

His tufted brows dropped a notch. "It's goin' to happen someday, White Magpie. That's why you got to watch her." He got to his feet with one hand on the saddle pole. "In the mornin' tell Luc to hitch up the buggy for me. I want to go see the old buffalo cow."

She arose, dusted off, and waited.

He said: "Let's go back to the house."

She walked beside him. When he had to pause before climbing the steps, she waited, close to him, and matched her stride to his as they mounted the steps. She steered him to a chair and hovered like a shriveled, wiry old bird until he was settled, then went inside to half fill a cup with whiskey and take it out to him.

He was asleep.

She took the cup back inside, then took Yellow Bluebell with her. They cleaned the old man's room, made his bed, and filled the nightstand pitcher with fresh water.

When the riders returned, Luc looked long in the direction of the main house before passing inside to care for his animal. He had something to tell the old man that he wished he did not have to say.

CHAPTER
SEVENTEEN

A Mourning Wolf

Luc ate at the bunkhouse. When he was finished, he loitered quietly for a while before going outside. The old man was in his chair on the porch. Someone had draped his sheep-pelt coat around his shoulders.

There were lights in the house which lacked the brilliance of those from the sky. There was not a cloud, and the hush was so deep that, when a wolf howled at the rising full moon which had a reddish tint, the sound that came from miles distant sounded as though it were just beyond the yard.

Luc crossed over and climbed the steps. The old man nodded. He had a bottle of whiskey on the railing near at hand. He said: "Set, boy. Whiskey, if you want it."

Luc sat and declined the whiskey which made the old man look at him. "The day will come," he predicted and rallied slightly under the coat. "Freeze hard tonight. Look at that sky."

Luc nodded without looking up.

Cameron said: "I'm goin' to take the buggy tomorrow an' visit the old buffalo. You could rig it out after breakfast."

Luc sat on the edge of his chair. "She's dead, Mister Cameron."

"Who's dead?"

"The buffalo cow."

"Cougar get her?"

"No. There's a tree near the creek where she bedded down an' sort of rested. She's leanin' against the tree. I'd guess she went to sleep an' just didn't wake up."

Cameron reached for the bottle, swallowed, and replaced it atop the railing. "The calf . . . ?"

"She's with some cows. I don't think she's had no milk for a long time. The calf didn't need her ma no more. She mostly grazes along with the cattle."

"I expect you better tell Yellow Bluebell."

Luc did not move. "I figured I'd take Ed and Sid with diggin' tools an' the dray wagon in the mornin'. Bury her by her tree."

Cameron faced Luc. "An' you figure I'll tell the girl?"

"No. I figured you'd tell the old woman, an' she can tell Yellow Bluebell."

The old man eventually nodded, lurched for the rail, gripped it, and pulled himself upright. He ignored the bottle. "There's somethin' that bothers me, Luc. If you was to leave . . . ?"

"I'm not goin' to leave, Mister Cameron," the younger man said as he also arose. "I been stayin' here because I'm fond of the place."

"That letter you took up yonder. It was my will. Everythin' goes to Yellow Bluebell. She don't know nothin' about a big cow outfit. Neither does the old woman. If you was to leave . . . ? I tell you what I'll do . . . double your rider's wages if you'll stay an' run things for 'em."

Luc nodded. "I'll stay."

The old man went to the door and spoke as he opened it. "Give the old buffalo a nice grave." He closed the door after himself.

White Magpie was sitting in the parlor, wizened and small in the old leather chair. She said: "Yellow Bluebell asleep."

He nodded.

She looked more lined and ancient in the lamplight. "You bed down," she told him. Although she did not mean to sound peremptory, that was how it came out. Cameron scowled at her. "Any hot coffee in the pot?"

She did not move. "No coffee. Too late."

He gazed at her for a moment, then said: "Good night."

She repeated it in Lakota.

When he had gone, White Magpie blew out the lamps. Because she did not like beds up off the ground with stuffed mattresses, she slept on the floor in Yellow Bluebell's room with a buffalo robe under her and a heavy Hudson's Bay blanket on top. But this night she did not bed down for a while. She sat in the chair until the fireplace burned down to coals, then slipped outside. Cold hit her face-on. She breathed deeply of it.

There were ragged old cottonwood trees, no pines or firs. There were outbuildings and the large log barn. There were corrals and pens. All things here were made to contain, to hold, to prevent freedom.

224

She went out to the corrals to smell horses and saw the old man's big sorrel solemnly regarding her. She spoke to the horse quietly in Lakota. The horse did not move. She told the sorrel her people ate big, slick horses. She told him of her grandfather who only saw white-eyed people when he was very old, ready to die. He had been a great warrior who killed many Crows. The horse finally moved away. As it moved, she said: "We be friends long time."

She wandered beyond the yard. It was cold. The big moon was high, pure silver now. The blanket behind it with all those moth holes let the light through from beyond.

She returned to the house where everything was dark, groped for her bedding, and went to sleep — to wait — but the white bird did not come. Not to her.

In the morning White Magpie was busy in the kitchen when Yellow Bluebell came. Their greeting was brief. Yellow Bluebell knew how to peel potatoes with a little knife and went to work in silence. Eventually she asked the old woman if the mother mouse would miss her as much as she missed the mother mouse. White Magpie was frying meat and did not turn when she replied in Crow: "She miss you while you were with her. Now, she has other friends."

The noise of a wagon leaving the yard drew Yellow Bluebell to a window. The old woman glanced askance without speaking.

They waited an hour for the old man. When he did not come, the old woman went soundlessly to his bedroom. She did not go beyond the door. She waited a long time before she began a trilling chant which brought Yellow Bluebell. The old woman stopped and said: "Long sleep."

The girl's eyes widened. "He is asleep?"

"Long sleep, Yellow Bluebell."

The girl ran from the house and did not stop until she was behind the barn where the using horses had been fed and were lipping up an occasional stalk. They paid no attention to her until she cried in her arms. It was a keening kind of sobbing. A horse or two looked up, listened, then went back to nuzzling for overlooked stalks.

White Magpie remained in the house. For lack of anything else to do she cleaned up the meal which had not been served, went out back to pile kindling, heard the girl out behind the barn, and went back inside to the bedroom doorway. She spoke in Lakota, softly and solemnly.

"Find Crow woman. Find baby. Knowing Spirit will show you good land with a creek an' trees, and Many-Horses. Someday your big red horse."

Yellow Bluebell did not return, but Luc and the hired hands did, with their tools in the dray wagon.

White Magpie waited. The day was spent. The sun was leaving. She went to the porch and sat in the old man's chair, which was where Luc saw her and started across the yard. He stopped on the last step. She met his gaze, showing nothing. He went closer. The only person he had ever seen use that particular chair was Mister Cameron.

226

White Magpie said: "In bedroom." She heard the door open and close at her back. She waited, not as long this time.

Luc came out, ignored the old woman, sank into a chair, and sat hunched. Someone shouted from behind the barn. No one answered him. The man christened Oswald but called Sid came out front now to call across the yard to Luc.

"Injun girl hurt down here."

Seeking a place where she would not be found, Yellow Bluebell had climbed to the loft, had crept over layers of hay to lie flat inside the loft door, which was tied open to aerate hay. She was still clutching the gold necklace with the engraved bird when Luc reached her. The old woman began a soft trilling.

Yellow Bluebell was unconscious when they carried her to the bed in the main house. White Magpie disapproved of their probing but kept still. The graying rider called Sid felt for broken bones, straightened up, and said: "If she landed flat out on her back, there's nothin' anyone can do."

She had been lying on her right side with one arm above her head when they had found her. Luc told the old woman to fetch whiskey, which White Magpie did but reluctantly. She had seen unconscious people many times. Indian custom was to make them comfortable, block out all light, and wait. White men used whiskey.

Sid propped up the girl. Luc trickled whiskey until she involuntarily swallowed, then choked, and coughed. White Magpie pushed the men away, wiped the girl's lips, and called the men several bad names in Crow. In

English she said: "You go!" and for emphasis raised a skinny, withered old arm in the direction of the door.

They went.

In the parlor they wondered what she had been doing in the loft. Luc shook his head and in silence led the way back to the yard.

After dusk passed, the riders lighted lamps in the bunkhouse. There was little conversation. To them it was difficult to understand anyone falling from the loft.

Because they had worked hard burying the old buffalo cow, they were hungry. If there'd been whiskey, they'd have had a drink, too, but there was none. In the morning they loitered at the barn until Luc said he would go to the main house. They watched him cross the yard and waited.

White Magpie opened the door and moved aside. In the parlor Luc asked how she was, and the old woman did not answer. She jerked her head and led the way to the bedroom.

Yellow Bluebell was propped up with a rolled blanket behind her. Her dark eyes were unwavering as Luc and the old woman entered. She said something Luc did not understand to which White Magpie replied in English: "Tell him."

Yellow Bluebell's dark gaze returned to Luc as she touched the gold necklace. "Father man to me," she said. "I don't want him to die." She held up the necklace. "He gave me this."

Luc went to a chair at bedside and sat down. "How do you feel? How did you happen to fall?"

White Magpie gestured. "She was cryin' too close to open place. She fall."

Luc turned his attention to the old woman. "Can she walk?"

"Yes. She sore."

Luc looked at Yellow Bluebell. "I expect she's sore. She's lucky she didn't break somethin'. Belle, don't never climb up there again."

She looked steadily at him without speaking or nodding.

Luc arose, facing the old woman. She said: "Put him beside Crow woman an' baby."

Luc knew the place. It had a little wooden fence around it to keep out cattle.

The old woman went as far as the parlor with him. "You come back?"

"Yes'm. Often as I can. How long you expect she'll be a-bed?"

"No long. Maybe tomorrow, maybe next day. You come back, bring flowers."

He stood a moment, eyeing the old woman, then left. At the barn the riders were waiting. He explained about Andrew Cameron. Neither of the riders was surprised, but they said nothing.

The digging tools were still in the wagon. They put the stud-necked big Oregon mare back into harness and drove to the place with the wooden fence. Sid spoke aside to his partner when Luc went back to the wagon. "Two graves in a row?"

Ed shrugged.

The digging was hard work. By the time they were finished and drove back to the yard, where Luc took care of the mare and the rangemen went to the bunkhouse, they were as hungry as a pair of bitch wolves. When Luc entered, they were preparing a meal. He said he'd be back directly and went to the main house where White Magpie admitted him. Yellow Bluebell was lighting lamps, which she stopped doing when she saw him. He wagged his head at her. She was embarrassed but did not flee.

White Magpie fixed him with a gimlet stare. "No flowers?"

"Tomorrow," he replied. "After we cover the grave. You two want to come to the buryin'?"

White Magpie said. "We come! We help cover hole!"

He considered Yellow Bluebell for a long moment before leaving. After his departure Yellow Bluebell sat down and the old woman raised a hand to her mouth as she said: "Knees go weak."

Yellow Bluebell reddened. She asked in Crow how the old woman knew about such things and got the answer in the same language.

"I sit down when my man come to visit the first time. That's how I know." White Magpie also said: "We make burial bundle. Come along. I show you."

The old man was no longer stiff, which made it easier when they moved him. The Indian custom was not to put people in the ground, but he was a white-eyes. They always put their dead in the ground. To White Magpie it made little difference. It was easier to put someone in a hole in the ground than to lift them in ceremonial robes to high wooden platforms.

When they had Cameron rolled and tied, Yellow Bluebell removed the gold necklace and placed it on his chest. White Magpie said nothing, but, when they went outside to the porch, she told the girl in Crow white people did not bury things with their dead.

Yellow Bluebell said: "I do."

That ended the conversation.

After full darkness White Magpie took the girl out beyond the limits of the yard where they sat in silence. The huge moon arrived, the moth-hole lights shone, and they had to wait a long time in the cold before the wolf sounded, very distantly. Not a mating call, a mourning cry.

White Magpie arose to head back when Yellow Bluebell said: "Where does he go?"

The old woman pointed skyward with a withered arm. "Behind the moon."

In the morning after the burial bundle had been loaded, Luc offered the women a ride. White Magpie shook her head. She and Yellow Bluebell would walk.

It was early, but, by the time they reached the fenced off place, let down the tailgate, and carried the old man inside, there was warmth. Not summer warmth because summer was past, but the sparkling clear warmth of an autumn day.

Luc considered the necklace after they lowered the old man and frowned.

White Magpie said: "She send it with him."

Sid and Ed went about the burial with solemn faces. They had not known the old man very long, but the circumstances were sobering. When the girl showed tears without making a sound, they avoided looking at her.

The women walked back behind the wagon. Sid asked Luc who those other two graves belonged to, and, because he did not know, Luc shook his head.

After supper Luc appeared at the main house to tell the women what the old man had told him: Yellow Bluebell now owned the A C Connected cow outfit. He also told them he had promised the old man he would stay to run the place.

White Magpie listened and nodded. When he left, she followed him to the porch and asked: "Where is flowers?"

He answered quietly. "Tomorrow. I'll take you both in the buggy so's you get an idea how big the place is, how many cattle there is. I'll give her some flowers then."

White Magpie's reply was slyly given. "Not me. I stay back. You take Yellow Bluebell."

"But you'd ought to know somethin' about . . ."

"No! She stay. Someday I be gone. I stay here. You take her. Remember flowers."

The old woman went to the door, glanced back once, went inside, and closed the door.

About the Author

Lauran Paine who, under his own name and various pseudonyms has written over 900 books, was born in Duluth, Minnesota. His family moved to California when he was at an early age and his apprenticeship as a Western writer came about through the years he spent in the livestock trade, rodeos, and even motion pictures — where he served as an extra because of his expert horsemanship in several films starring movie cowboy Johnny Mack Brown. In the late 1930s, Paine trapped wild horses in northern Arizona and, for a time, worked as a professional farrier. Paine came to know the old West through the eyes of many who had been born in the previous century and he learned that Western life had been very different from the way it was portrayed on the screen. "I knew men who had killed other men," he later recalled. "But they were the exceptions. Prior to and during the Depression, people were just too busy eking out an existence to indulge in Saturday-night brawls." He served in the U.S. Navy in the Second World War and began writing for Western pulp magazines following his discharge. It is interesting to note that all of his earliest novels (written under his own name and the pseudonym Mark Carrel) were published in the British market and he soon had as strong a following in that country as in the United States. Paine's Western fiction is characterized by strong plots, authenticity, an apparently effortless ability to construct situation and character, and a preference for building his stories upon a solid foundation of historical fact. *Adobe Empire* (1956), one of his best novels, is a fictionalized account of the last twenty years in the life of trader William Bent and, in an off-trail way, has a melancholy, bittersweet texture that is not easily forgotten. In later novels like *The White Bird* (1997) and *Cache Cañon* (1998), he showed that the special magic and power of his stories and characters had only matured along with his basic themes of changing times, changing attitudes, learning from experience, respecting Nature, and the yearning for a simpler, more moderate way of life. The film *Open Range* (Buena Vista, 2003), based on Paine's 1990 novel, starring Robert Duvall, Kevin Costner, and Annette Bening became an international success.